HOMECOMING
HEI$T

TYSON COLLIN

HOMECOMING HEI$T

atmosphere press

TABLE OF CONTENTS

CHAPTER 1

DESPERATE TIMES

It was a cool, crisp morning in Steamboat, Missouri. The perfect mix of cold air above the warm water from the creek created the season's first fog. Morning Park walkers enjoyed the lifting precipitation off the waterway that ran through town. In the town, two new bridges gave access, making the old landmark bridge the new pedestrian trail pathway.

Steamboat is a small town, often referred to as the 'City of Pride' by the locals. As such, it thrived on small businesses— diners, railroad shops, and construction companies. One of the more popular construction firms operated out of a small trailer parked temporarily on a plot of land on the south end of town. The owner had even gone as far as creating a small parking lot in front of his quaint office. It really gave off a homey feel.

The owner of the trailer, the head of the construction company, was none other than Bo Foster. The trailer had two compartments, the main office and a small meeting room by the entrance. Bo's office was quite simple. It consisted of a large mahogany desk and a single bookshelf. Beside his desk was a window with a clear view of the parking lot and the surrounding wooded area.

Bo sat behind his desk that lovely fall day, his nose deep in a newspaper and his legs folded over his desk. Bo's face could be described as chiseled with medium cocoa skin. He had a prominent jawline, covered with rough stubble that stopped just below his ear. His hair was cut was high and tight. Bo preferred business casual clothing and had on a white shirt over brown dress pants.

Suddenly, the cellular on Bo's desk started ringing. He sat up and reached for it quickly with hope in his expression.

"Good day. I've been waiting for your call."

Bo set down his paper and leaned back in his seat with a loud sigh.

"Please, tell me you have good news."

He fell silent and nodded his head along to the voice on the other side of the line. Bo's expression went through three stages. He started chipper, then his smile deflated a little, and finally, his eyes lost their shine. Bo nodded solemnly.

"Alright, I understand. Thanks for the call and take care of yourself."

Bo gently returned the phone to the desktop and stared at it for a few seconds as he tried to process what he had heard. He picked up his newspaper and tried to resume his reading, but the worry building up within him impeded his concentration.

Bo put the paper down once more and covered his face with his hands as he sighed. He took a moment to steady his breathing and tried to psyche himself up.

"Come on! You've faced tougher situations than this."

As he was speaking, the phone rang again. Bo didn't need to check the caller ID to know who it was. He dreaded picking up the call and let the phone ring for a few seconds. It persisted, and finally, he caved and picked up the phone.

"Hello?"

Bo tried his best to steady his voice, but some of his nervousness came through. He recognized the banker's voice as a reply came through.

"Hi, Bo. It's me. I was just calling to check in on that deal we talked about the other day."

Bo's shoulders slumped and he rested his elbows against the desk as he responded.

"The client just called to cancel the contract. She backed out before we could finalize things."

The banker sighed on the other side of the line, and Bo could picture him massaging the bridge of his nose.

"I thought this was a done deal, Bo? You seemed pretty sure of yourself when we talked earlier."

Bo nodded to no one in particular.

"They decided on a cheaper alternative. I tried my best."

Bo could hear the banker settling into his seat and knew a fierce argument was near.

"Our deal was that you wouldn't take a single penny from your next four houses. Surely, you can understand my concern for one of those deals falling through."

Bo felt anger rising deep within him and raised his voice slightly as he replied.

"I know that. But my last two contractors insisted on being paid what they owe. They threatened to issue liens and hold up the buildings, so I had to follow through."

Bo shook his head.

"My hands were tied."

Bo took a deep breath and dropped his volume.

"Look, nothing has changed. I just need a little more time."

Silence met his response. Bo knew his caller well enough to understand what that meant.

"I already gave you more time a year ago. Remember? Look, you and I go way back. We've known each other, what? Fifteen, seventeen years. But this is pushing it."

Bo replied calmly.

"Exactly my point. You know me better than most. You know I honor my commitments. I'm good at it. I just need a little more patience on your part."

The banker replied immediately.

"But what about the things outside of your control?"

Bo massaged one of his temples while he listened.

"The market is turning into a horror fest. I've never seen it this bad. Even the guys on the board are shaken, and they went through the madness of the mid-'70s and the late 2000s."

Bo sank back in his seat.

"Ok."

The banker went on.

"We have the highest number of recalls the bank has seen in the last two years. We are a bank that lends, but the market has us looking like a realty firm. I spend most of my time talking to clients, listing out foreclosures. It's so damn frustrating."

Bo sighed and nodded.

"Alright, I hear you. You don't have it easy either. Look, just give me a final date on the outstanding properties, and we can work from there. Does that sound good?"

The banker grunted.

"Sure. But you won't like it. I'll call you later."

Bo nodded and returned the phone to the desktop. He glared at the phone for a few seconds, and rage flared to life in his eyes. Bo cleared his desk in a single swipe, sending all his documents and instruments flying all over the place. He sighed and leaned against the empty desk with his hands on his head.

⊕

Doug Harris walked into his garage, armed with a wrench. His home had seen better days and was one of the many older buildings still standing in Steamboat. The paint was cracked and faded beyond recognition, but it might have been blue at some point. The place was a single-story bungalow, and the garage was detached and further into the yard.

Doug looked about as beaten up as his home. His hair fell just short of his jaw and had strands of gray mixed in. His eyes were sunken and his forehead wrinkled. Doug grunted as he approached a younger man hunched over a car.

"Hey, kid. See if this works."

Doug handed the tool over to Steve, his nephew. Steve was as scruffy looking as his uncle, with dark brown hair that stopped just over his shoulders. His beard was a lot fuller. His mustache, on the other hand, was a bit less.

The pair stood before a beaten-up old station wagon with a workbench just to the left of the open engine. Steve tested the weight of the wrench in his hand and furrowed his eyebrows.

"Is this the right size?"

Doug walked right past Steve and made a beeline for the beer on the workbench. He popped it open and took a big swig before replying.

"How the hell should I know? Why don't you try it and find out?"

Doug gently pushed Steve's head away as he waltzed by, and the latter sighed before bending over the engine to begin work. He focused on the problem bolt next to the radiator and began tightening it. The wrench seemed to fit just fine, and his tension eased once he was in a steady rhythm.

Doug continued to enjoy his beer, and he mellowed slightly once the buzz began to kick in. He leaned against the car and stared out of the garage as he spoke.

"You know, seeing you hunched over that engine like that reminds me a lot of your father."

Doug turned to Steve and went on.

"He and I used to work on cars like this when we were just

teenagers."

Doug smiled as the memories came flooding in.

"Any engine we could get our hands on."

Steve grunted as he continued to work on the engine.

"Yeah. There was always a car in every picture of him mom bothered to keep around."

Doug nodded and took another swig of his beer.

"Yes, sir. There was nothing your father and I couldn't figure out. As long as it had an engine, we would eventually have it roaring to life."

Doug laughed heartily and drank from his beer.

"We were also fiercely competitive back then. Your dad and I would occasionally clash to determine who could fix an engine faster or better. There was no end to our shenanigans."

Doug turned his attention to the sky outside the garage doors and went on.

"Your dad was easily the more spirited one. He even tried to race one time."

Steve looked up from his work in surprise.

"I never heard that one before. Are you serious?"

Doug nodded and burped.

"Very."

Steve turned to the engine and went back to work.

"Mom never said anything about that."

Doug grunted and nodded.

"I would have been shocked if she did. Your mamma didn't care much about the races. She was afraid he would kill himself trying to win."

Steve paused as he responded.

"Well, it didn't matter in the end. He got wrapped up with the wrong crowd and still ended up dead."

Steve shrugged.

"A person has got to die sometime, right? Besides, mom didn't talk about him much. I guess she was too embarrassed?"

Doug eyed Steve from the corner of his eyes and grunted.

"Well, let me try to fill you in on a little bit of family history. Your daddy ended up meeting someone that taught him a thing or two about racing."

Doug sighed and went on.

"Call it luck or whatever you wish. The result was his fierce determination to be a race car driver. Despite his obvious lack of experience."

Doug stared at his feet.

"We all tried to talk him out of it, but your dad didn't want to hear it. He was determined to make it to the Winston Cup and race with the big boys. One way or another."

Steve looked up as he wiped his hand with a rag.

"I didn't know that. Did he make it?"

Doug turned to Steve and shook his head.

"But wouldn't it have been a great story if he did?"

Steve returned, gathered all the tools into the toolbox, and carried it to the back of the garage.

"I'm not a fan of fairytales."

He returned to the engine and stared down at his work in satisfaction.

"All done."

Doug acknowledged his declaration with a curt nod and downed what was left of his beer.

"Your father never made it to NASCAR. But I can't say he didn't try."

Doug placed the empty bottle on the workbench and went on.

"His biggest accomplishment was a couple of races down at the county dirt track. All that ended during the championship race. He always said he would take the prize money and buy him and your mom an older muscle car. She liked the ones that had the stripes down the center."

Doug gazed off into the distance.

"I remember it like it was yesterday. He was giving those

pros a run for their money and was right on the ass of the first-place driver."

Doug shook his head.

"Unfortunately, the driver behind him wasn't going to take that sitting down. At the last turn, they sent your dear dad flying off the track. His car flipped onto its roof and slid to a halt."

Doug sighed, and his expression mellowed.

"He wasn't the same after that. Part of him died on that track. What was left was just a shadow of his former self. That was when he got involved with some shady characters over in Illinois."

Steve turned bitter and glared at his clenched fist.

"I hope it was worth it."

CHAPTER 2

SLIPPERY SLOPE

Doug quickly sensed the bitterness in Steve's words. He thought of what had happened following his brother's incident and sighed.

"Look, you have every right to be angry. A boy is meant to grow up with a father in his life."

Doug shook his head.

"It's just one of the many times I felt disappointed in your father."

Doug stood a reasonable distance away from Steve and stared at the empty bottle on the workbench. His vision swam, but he fought to focus as he spoke.

"You were dealt a tough hand, but I tried to do right by you. Especially when your mom passed."

Steve's anger was quickly replaced by sadness. The corners of his eyes drooped, and he deflated.

"I wanted to keep you, but you have to understand."

Doug clenched his fist as he went on.

"My record wasn't exactly spotless. I had two stints in jail. No judge in their right mind would give a kid to an ex-con.

Especially considering your father's criminal past. Your mom's passing of cancer is the hardest thing we've ever had to deal with."

Steve sunk into a seat and sighed. He twiddled his thumbs against each other and focused on his feet.

"You're telling me? After that, it was a foster home after foster home. I never stayed in one place long enough to make any real friends or warm up to a family."

Steve shook his head.

"It wasn't easy, I tell ya."

Doug grunted and walked closer.

"It didn't help that you dropped out of school, or that you started selling drugs and getting into the same trouble your father did."

Doug's expression mellowed, and his tone dropped.

"You could have made something of yourself."

Steve glared at his uncle as he rose from his seat. He pushed past him and responded.

"You know what they say. The apple doesn't fall far from the tree."

Doug stood his ground as Steve left the garage. The place fell silent as the sunset, allowing him to reflect in peace.

⌗

The day was quickly drawing to an end. Businesses started to close, and people headed home for the day. Bo stared at the clock in his office and watched the time go by. The day had been relatively slow, and besides a few phone calls and some paperwork, he didn't have much to do.

Quitting time arrived, and Bo got up to close for the day. He organized his files so he wouldn't have trouble sorting through them the next day. Once Bo ensured the windows were shut, he grabbed his hat and headed out of the exit.

Bo drove up to the area's only lumber company, one of his

favorite suppliers. Bo had been good friends with the owner for quite some time and intended to speak to him that evening. Bo walked into the building and headed straight for the counter.

"Hey there, Todd."

Todd looked up from his desk and smiled. He had a bald head and, around it, a crown of gray and brown hair. Todd was on the portly side and had wrinkles on his forehead. He radiated a warmth that worked wonders on Bo's mental state.

"Hey, Bo. It's been a while."

Todd got up with some effort and shook Bo's hand over the counter.

"Glad to see you're still alive and kicking."

Todd laughed heartily before responding.

"Likewise."

He settled into his seat and went on.

"So, how have you been?"

Bo laughed drily and shook his head.

"The usual; bankers thinking they're real estate agents."

Todd furrowed his eyebrows and clicked his tongue.

"That bad, huh?"

Bo sighed and forced a smile.

"It's fine. Things will work out."

Todd nodded his head.

"I have faith in you."

A sly grin appeared on Bo's face, and he spoke up.

"You could help make things better by buying a house."

Todd chuckled and shook his head.

"You only get the one, I'm afraid. Brenda and I are just fine with the place you built for us back in '06. Still standing firm."

Todd smiled from ear to ear as he went on.

"It would be silly to move out now."

Bo nodded.

"Yeah, I know. Figured it was worth a shot anyway."

He leaned against the counter and kept his eyes fixed on

his fingers as Todd spoke up.

"So, what brings you to this side of town? Did you miss me?"

Bo traced lines on the counter as he replied.

"Of course, I did. I figured I'd come to check up on you."

He rapped his fingers rhythmically and went on.

"Also, I wanted to make sure that you're still fine with what we discussed a few weeks ago."

Todd nodded slowly.

"Yup, definitely. Has anything changed since then?"

Bo's worries bubbled to the forefront. He scratched his head and sighed.

"A little bit. I owe you for six houses. I still can't figure out how it got that bad."

Bo shook his head slowly.

"Anyways, I've closed on one, and I have another closing at the end of the month."

Todd clapped his palms together and leaned back in his seat with a smile.

"That's excellent news."

Bo folded his arms and slowly shook his head.

"It's bittersweet, I'm afraid. I just had a couple walk out on me earlier today. Something about a cheaper alternative and two contractors threatened to issue liens. They went back on our deal at the worst possible time."

Todd whistled softly.

"All that in a week? That's terrible."

Bo laughed drily and shook his head.

"A week? I wish. All that in the last three days."

Todd extended his sympathies.

"That's sounds tough."

Bo nodded.

"Anyways, I came down here to talk to you, man to man. A message or a phone call would have been too impersonal. I appreciate all you've done for me so far, and I'd really appreciate it if you could stick with me a little longer."

Todd nodded aggressively.

"Of course. I helped you start this business. I'm going to see it through. Count on that."

Bo took Todd's hand in a firm handshake and smiled.

"That takes a load off. Please, still send an email with the total and breakdown. I want to make sure I have the right numbers."

Todd nodded, and Bo turned to leave.

"Thanks again. Have a good evening."

With that said, he exited the building.

⊞

The exterior of Doug's home was outmatched only by the interior. His living room looked dark and dingy with worn-out furniture dotted across the room. The center of attention was an old couch positioned before an old TV. The couch was flanked on the left by an easy chair and on the right by a smaller chair with the same ratty material.

Steve sat in front of the TV, enjoying a football rerun. Doug walked into the room and gently reclined on the easy chair with a loud sigh. He had a beer in hand and placed it on the center table before him.

"Is there anything good on?"

Steve replied with a grunt. Doug sighed and cracked open his beer.

"Glad we were able to get that old station wagon running."

Steve lifted a single eyebrow and turned on his uncle.

"We?"

Doug sighed.

"Kids these days. Never showing appreciation. So, now that you've got a set of working wheels think you'll get steady work?"

Doug took a sip from his beer while he listened to his

nephew's response.

"I'll look, that's for sure. But I wouldn't count on getting anything good."

Steve shrugged. Doug sighed and shook his head.

"Of course you won't! Not with that attitude, anyway. Where's that positive can-do spirit?"

Steve grunted.

"In a children's book. Why do you always pick on me?"

Doug reached out and ruffled Steve's hair.

"Because if I don't, who will?"

He took another sip of his beer and sighed with satisfaction. Steve ran his fingers through his long locks and set every strand back in place before going on.

"As I said, I'll look. Bo is my best bet. He really came through last time. I'll head on down and see if he has anything for me."

Doug paused with his beer inches from his mouth, and his ears perked up.

"Who's Bo?"

"He runs a construction company in the next town. I ran a power washer job for him a while back."

Steve shrugged.

"He asked if I was interested in part-time work, and that was it."

Steve had managed to capture Doug's attention.

"Does he pay well?"

Steve considered the question carefully.

"Well enough. He pays in cash, so I can't complain."

Doug stroked his chin as he processed the information offered by Steve. His eyes came alive, and he spoke.

"Well, if he needs two guys, put in a good word for me."

Steve chuckled.

"I don't think he needs his car fixed."

Doug feigned hurt and scoffed.

"It may not look like it, but I know a thing or two about

carpentry. Just don't forget to mention me. The rest will sort itself out."

Steve sighed.

"I thought you had your own thing at the scrapyard. Small engine repairs and whatnot."

Doug growled gently and glared at Steve.

"Don't you worry about what I got going on. Just do as I asked."

Steve held his hand up in surrender.

"Okay, jeez."

He got up from his seat and shook his head as he headed out of the room.

"Where are you going?"

Steve paused and glared over his shoulder.

"To the kitchen."

"Get me a beer while you're at it."

Steve sighed and massaged the bridge of his nose.

"I swear, you're going to kill yourself one day. Aren't you meant to be going to AA meetings?"

Steve continued to grumble as he disappeared into the kitchen.

⌗

Steamboat was a small town a stone's throw away from St. Louis, Missouri. It was a quaint little town that thrived on small businesses. Some of the town's attractions included a rail yard memorial with tracks leading to and from it. Other attractions included many of the county's best parks and, jokingly with some of the locals, the longest one-sided Main Street in the state. The Melba movie theater with a '60s style marquee sign above the entrance, the city police station, built from red brick, and the town's high school, home of their beloved football team.

Steamboat may not have been flashy, but it was homey,

and the locals loved it. It was a lovely afternoon. A warm fall breeze rustled the foliage that flanked the streets. That afternoon, an AA meeting was scheduled to hold in an empty office in a small plaza off Main in downtown Steamboat.

A collection of chairs was arranged in a large circle at the center of the room. A few minutes to the agreed meeting time, a man walked into the room. He had on a classic gray suit from the 1980s with an open striped white shirt. His black hair was slicked back and reflected the little light that trickled into the room. Phil Sexton had been working with struggling alcoholics for quite some time and knew the drill.

Naturally, he was the first to arrive, but people began to flock in one after the other once the agreed time arrived. The dedicated were the first to arrive, followed closely by the coerced and capped off by the stragglers. Phil stared each of the men and women in the eye as they filed in and took note of their mental states as they sat.

A big part of his job was trying to help those struggling to quit their addictions cold turkey. It wasn't the easiest job in the world, but it had its ups.

Phil patiently waited for the room to fill up. Those present began to converse with one another. Another reason for the gatherings was to allow people to share their experiences. It helps to have someone that understands.

Five minutes had gone by since the beginning of the meeting, and Phil figured it was a good time to start. He got up and put on his brightest smile.

"Hey guys, welcome to Alcoholics Anonymous. Shall we begin?"

CHAPTER 3

PREMEDITATED SCHEMING

The AA meeting ran its course and soon drew to a close.

"Well, that's all the time we have for today. I'm glad you all could make it and am glad to hear of your progress and thanks for sharing. Same time next week. Until then, stay safe."

The gathering dispersed. Some of the attendants couldn't wait to get out of the room, but some lingered to discuss further. Phil was accommodating to those that lingered, and eventually, they left.

Phil was locked in a conversation with one of the attendants as they stepped out of the entrance.

"I'm glad to see you're determined to beat this. We'll talk more next week: if not, I urge you to reach out to your sponsor before then."

The man nodded and took Phil's hand in a firm handshake.

"Thanks for all the help."

Doug watched the interaction from afar under the shade of a nearby tree. He waited until Phil was on his own before approaching.

"Long time, no see."

Phil jumped slightly and sighed once he noticed who was talking.

"Damnit, Doug. You startled me."

Phil smiled and extended his hand.

"Yeah, it has been. How have you been?"

Doug shrugged.

"I've been alright. Keeping busy."

Phil's smile deflated a little.

"Is that why you've been missing AA meetings?"

Doug sighed and ran his fingers through his hair.

"Sorry about that."

Phil lifted a single eyebrow.

"You relapsed, didn't you?"

Doug's guilty look was the only reply Phil needed.

"Come on, Doug."

Doug held his hands up.

"Look, I've been doing some thinking, and I'm not sure the sober life is for me."

He shrugged and went on.

"I mean, it's not like I had much of a problem in the first place. I'm more of a social drinker. So, I have a couple of beers once in a while. So, what?"

Phil sighed and slowly shook his head.

"Alright, then. So, what brings you here?"

Doug smiled and placed a reassuring hand on Phil's shoulder.

"The past. Do you have time to talk?"

Phil sensed the subject was delicate and slowly nodded.

"We might as well grab a bite to eat in the process. How about the usual diner? My treat."

Doug's eyes lit up.

"Sounds like a plan."

The pair walked off, side by side.

✛

The Main Street Diner had been established in the '70s. Despite its inability to evolve with the times, it remained a local favorite and served some of the best food in Steamboat. Doug and Phil walked into the diner and found an empty booth at the back. A waitress walked up to their table with a bright smile and a pen poised over a writing pad.

"Good evening, gentlemen. What are you in the mood for?"

The pair gave their orders. Doug and Phil sat silently until the waitress returned with the coffee they ordered.

"Your food will be out in a minute. Enjoy."

Doug took a sip from his cup and sighed.

"It's been a while since I visited this place. I see they still make amazing coffee."

Phil nodded and smiled.

"The food is always great."

He turned to Doug and went on.

"So, what did you want to talk about?"

Doug set down his mug and stared at the brown liquid.

"When we first started AA, you said something that really stuck with me. You said some of us would make it out of this phase with time, some of us would keep stumbling, and some of us would never make it."

Phil nodded.

"I remember that. I was trying to be as real as possible. In hindsight, that might not have been the most encouraging thing to say."

He laughed nervously and rubbed the back of his head. Doug shook his head in disagreement.

"You spoke the truth. I like to think I'm a little bit of all three cases melded together."

Phil took a sip of his coffee and sighed.

"And why is that?"

"Well, look at my track record. I drink every single day, but I do it moderately. I never get blackout drunk. Also, if I've managed to stay off the stuff for a couple of weeks, I turn up at AA meetings."

Phil listened attentively, trying to fish out a problem like he was trained to.

"I see. Well, you seem to have everything under control."

He turned to Doug and went on.

"But if that ever changes, don't hesitate to call me."

Doug met Phil's gaze, and the latter noticed a sparkle in the former's eyes.

"There's another way you can help me."

"Oh? What would that be?"

Their waitress returned as Doug was about to respond, and he paused. The lady set down their meals and left with a kind smile on her face.

"Freedom."

Phil was clearly confused.

"Freedom from what?"

Doug tapped his head lightly.

"The thoughts swirling through my head. Some nights, I'm not even able to sleep. I try to forget, but it lingers, waiting for me to drop my guard."

Doug turned to Phil with a severe expression on his face.

"Do you ever think, what if?"

Phil's expression was guarded as he responded.

"You can't be talking about..."

Doug nodded, and that earned a groan from Phil.

"You know I don't like talking about it. If that's all you dragged me here for, then I might as well leave."

Doug shook his head and held out his hands.

"I know I'm asking a lot, but humor me for a second."

Phil noticed the sincerity in Doug's eyes, and that calmed him down considerably. He sighed and sunk back into his seat. Doug took a bite from his eggs and paused.

"I did time, too, you know. And I remember what it was like behind bars. I thought of every decision I made that led up to me being incarcerated. I always thought of how I fucked up and what I could have done differently."

Doug sighed and shook his head.

"It isn't exactly a healthy mind frame. But have you ever imagined, what if...".?

Phil took over.

"What if we didn't get caught?"

Phil clenched his fists, and his expression reflected pain.

"We would still be out there with no idea where we're headed. Still constantly looking over our shoulders and not knowing who to trust."

Phil shook his head.

"I don't know about you, but that doesn't sound like a life worth living anymore. So, yeah. I'm glad I got caught. I mean, look at me now. No worries, no problems."

Doug rolled his eyes.

"Alright, I get you. Excuse me for asking a question. I was just curious."

Phil sighed.

"Look. Jail time should have been enough for you to reflect on your actions. We all got that extra time to think about our mistakes and what we could have done differently. Jail is all good and fine, but what matters the most is what you do after. The same thing goes for the AA."

Doug twiddled his thumbs, still deep in thought.

"Look, not all of us can choose our paths. Some of us were dealt a bad hand from the get-go and just need to follow through. I can't help that I think of what things used to be like in the good ol' days when it was just you and me."

Phil massaged the bridge of his nose with his thumb and forefinger. He took a moment to calm his nerves before getting up.

"Look, you and I have a lot of history. But I don't want that history to repeat itself. So, I'm just going to leave before this goes any further."

Phil grabbed a couple of singles from his wallet and tossed them down on the counter.

"This should pay for the food. Enjoy."

Doug nodded.

"Take care."

Phil waved over his shoulder and pushed through the exit. Doug watched him retreat to his car in disappointment as he sipped from his coffee.

The following day started like any other in this small community. The gray hair club walked their usual route down Main Street as they waved to the former sports star Andy in his patrol car. Andy had made his name popular with the locals with his athletic ability during his high school years. Now he gets to relive most of them with daily stops at one of the local shops or gas station, always smiling and glad to catch up with someone who used to watch him play. On the outskirts of town this day, Steve got up earlier than usual and made his way over to Steamboat. He decided to make good on his word and check in with Bo. Steve parked the beat-up station wagon in front of Bo's truck and stared at it for a second before stepping out. Steve approached the trailer and paused at the foot of the steps when he noticed Bo walking out.

"I was about to check who parked in my lot. Hey, Steve."

"Hey, Bo. It's just me."

Bo nodded.

"I can see that. What happened to that old truck you used to drive?"

Steve shrugged.

"It finally gave up. It was long overdue for changing anyways."

Bo folded his hands and nodded.

"I guess. So, what brings you to these parts?"

"Well, I figured I'd check in to see if you have any work for me."

Bo sighed and slowly shook his head.

"You didn't need to come all the way out here for that. I said I'd call if I have anything for you."

Steve smiled weakly.

"Well, I figured it wouldn't hurt to check."

Bo sighed, rubbed the back of his head.

"Look, I can understand that you might need the work, but I really don't have anything at the moment. I need to sell three more houses before I can really start something else. Or I'd need to stumble into a pot of gold before that happens."

Steve furrowed his eyebrows.

"Things are tough on this end too, huh?"

Bo sighed.

"To put it simply, yes. Everyone is worried about the market. People are going back on agreements, and I'm losing contracts. Handshakes don't mean anything anymore. It's really frustrating."

Steve nodded.

"I hear ya."

Bo looked up and went on.

"You wouldn't know anyone looking to buy a house, would you?"

Steve quickly shook his head.

"I don't know anyone that could afford the kind of houses you build."

Bo nodded slowly.

"Well, it was worth a shot. I'm asking everyone I run into. I'm bound to get a new client eventually."

Bo clapped Steve on the shoulder.

"Thanks for stopping by."

Steve figured it was time for him to leave.

"Glad I could talk to you. Also, if a job is ever available, please don't hesitate to call."

Bo nodded and watched as the beat-up old station wagon pulled out of the parking lot.

⊕

Doug frowned at the driveway from his seat in the garage.

"Where did this kid wander off to?"

Steve had been gone for quite some time, and Doug had no idea where to start looking. He perked up when he heard the sound of tires on gravel and watched as his nephew pulled into the driveway.

Steve parked just in front of the garage and stepped out of the vehicle.

"For God's sake, where have you been all day?"

Steve looked up with a startled expression.

"I did say I was heading out to look for a job."

Doug calmed a little.

"Oh, yeah. Did you find anything?"

Steve frowned.

"Well, I checked up with Bo."

Doug waited for a continuation, but none came.

"And?"

Steve shrugged.

"He didn't have any work."

He chuckled and went on.

"Heck, it seems he's hard up on cash as well. Asked me if I knew anyone looking to buy a house."

Steve captured Doug's interest.

"Did he outrightly say he was looking for money?"

Steve chuckled, thinking his uncle was joking. He paused when he noticed the severe expression on Doug's face.

"No, it was more of a joke. He said something about stumbling into a pot of gold or something like that."

Doug leaned forward in earnest.

"Were those his exact words?"

Steve eyed Doug suspiciously.

"Why are you so interested in what he had to say?"

Doug shrugged and settled back into his seat.

"Well, I've been working on an idea. It's still pretty rough so far, so I'm trying to put the pieces together."

Steve's interest was aroused, and he plopped down on an old cooler.

"Sounds interesting. Tell me about this idea."

Doug eyed the cooler and spoke.

"Toss me a beer, and I'll tell you all about it."

Steve reached into the cooler and tossed Doug a cold one before settling in to hear his story.

CHAPTER 4

CAREFUL SCHEMING

Walther Park was a lot less crowded than usual. The asphalt paths were littered with orange and brown leaves, carried about by sudden gusts of dry air. The lack of people made it easier to single out Phil, seated on a park bench. His expression was blank, and it was easy to tell that he was lost in thought.

The trees surrounding him rustled, snapping him out of his haze. Phil sighed and massaged his temple with one hand while reaching into his shirt pocket with the other. He retrieved a small notebook and leafed through the pages, pausing at a red marked page at the end.

Phil glanced over what was written and nodded to himself.

He closes his eyes. He went back to the '80s seeing himself sitting in a parked car in an alleyway, constantly looking over his shoulder. The anticipation within the vehicle was electrifying, and Phil had no idea what to expect next. The bank alarm went off, drawing Phil's attention to the building. Time seemed to crawl by and Phil's patience was stretched thin. Doug finally exited the building, but to his surprise, his partner steered clear of the car. A police car stopped in the middle of the street blocking Phil's only path of escape. Both officers stepped out of the cruiser, hands on their holsters as they slowly approached Phil's car. Doug saw this and skirted down the alley behind the bank. The memory faded and Phil returned to the present.

His eyes were oddly focused, and his resolve returned.

"I know what I need to do."

With that said, he slammed the small notebook shut.

⊕

Bo was hard at work at the crack of dawn. By late morning, his desk was swamped with files and documents, and there seemed to be no end in sight. Bo was determined to make some progress in drafting out new contracts. He was in the zone and the quiet of his trailer helped keep him calm.

The silence was broken by two sharp knocks that echoed through the small compartment. Bo looked up in frustration and slammed his pen into his table.

"So much for concentration."

He took a deep breath to calm himself and slowly got up from his table. Bo stalked off to the entrance and opened up. He came face to face with a somewhat frazzled looking individual. Bo's initial inclination was to believe that his guest was lost. That was quickly dispelled once the stranger confidently walked in.

"Hey there. Are you the man that builds houses?"

Bo was a bit surprised by the brash description of his job. But he quickly recovered.

"Yes, that's me."

He ushered his guest to the meeting room and offered him a seat.

"How can I help you? Are you interested in building a place?"

Doug shook his head slowly, but never broke eye contact.
"Not really."

Bo was clearly confused.

"How did you find out about this place?"

Doug smiled.

"Steve told me about you. He holds you in high regard."

Bo scratched the top of his head.

"I know a lot of Stevens. Could you be more specific?"

Doug snapped his fingers as he thought of a way to better describe his nephew.

"I believe he fixed a power washer for you not too long ago."

Bo's eyes widened.

"Oh, that Steve. Great kid."

Doug nodded in agreement.

"He came here a couple of days ago looking for work. For himself and me."

Bo became confused once more and slowly shook his head.

"I wasn't aware that he was asking for two people. Look, I have no idea what he told you. But I'm not currently in the market for new employees."

Doug held up his hands.

"I know; that the kid told me. I was hoping maybe I can help you and at the same time help me."

Bo had to admit that he was a little intrigued. He decided to push for some more information.

"And how do you plan to do that?"

Doug leaned closer with a sinister smile on his face.

"I heard you need quite a bit of money. If you're interested, I happen to know how you can get your hands on some."

Something about Doug's tone didn't sit right with Bo.

"Look, I don't know what Steve told you, but I'm not looking for any help with cash. I'm perfectly comfortable with my financial situation."

Doug raised a single eyebrow as he responded.

"Oh? Then it wasn't you that was hoping to stumble into a pot of gold?"

Bo chuckled and slowly shook his head.

"I see. I think there's a small misunderstanding here. I meant that as a joke. Steve must have taken it seriously."

Doug's smile deflated.

"Oh, I see."

Bo nodded.

"If you aren't looking to build a house, then I'm afraid I can't help you. Sorry to have wasted your time."

Doug eyed Bo closely for a moment. Content with what he saw, he nodded and got up from his seat.

"I see. I must have misunderstood then. Sorry to bother you."

He walked over to the exit and paused.

"I'll talk it over with Steve, then. Have a good day."

Doug shut the door behind him, plunging the room into silence. Bo could hear his heart beating frantically and took a moment to calm himself. Once he felt calmer, he took a deep breath, walked over to the window, and watched as Doug drove away.

James and Junk was the nearest scrapyard for miles. The place contained a large number of disposed of items, organized in several uneven piles. Later that day, Doug pulled into the junkyard in the old station wagon with Steve sitting in the passenger seat.

Doug felt right at home, driving into the junkyard. He had been working there for quite some time and knew the place inside and out. He skillfully maneuvered between the piles and drew to a stop near the west side.

Doug and Steve hopped out of the vehicle, and the first thing the former did was backtrack to the trunk and grab a beer. Doug pulled open the stopper and sighed as the light brown liquid fizzled.

"There we go."

Steve stared at the trash pile in front of them in awe. That particular pile seemed to be fenced off, and that piqued his curiosity. Doug reappeared with a beer in hand and stood beside his nephew.

"Pretty, isn't it?"

Steve eyed the stack of destroyed items and furrowed his eyebrows.

"Pretty isn't the word I would use. So, why are we here?"

Doug took a sip of his beer and sighed.

"You'll see. Follow me and watch your step."

Steve started to notice a theme as they drew nearer to the pile. It seemed to be a dedicated car graveyard. He noticed vehicles, long forgotten, and piled up in different manners. Some were stacked on top of each other. Others were lined in a row. Some were parked at odd angles and with no discernable patterns. For someone working in automobile repair, it was like stepping into heaven.

"Kid. Are you still here?"

Steve snapped back to the present and stared at Doug. He noticed Doug walking towards a break in the fence and followed.

"Don't get your clothes snagged on the sharp edges. The good stuff is around back. Follow me."

Doug and Steve faced a beaten path and walked for a reasonable distance before coming to a halt. Doug finished his beer and tossed it to the side before taking note of where they were. He faced a car blocking off a small passage and hopped over it.

Steve watched his uncle move on in confusion.

"Well, don't just stand there. Come on over."

Steve was soon standing next to Doug and eyed their surroundings.

"I still haven't seen anything impressive. Are you sure about this?"

Doug nodded and walked over to a set of cars backing the other side of the fence.

"I've been working on this for quite some time now."

He paused in front of the vehicles and gestured at them with a showman's flair.

"Is that it?"

Steven didn't look all that impressed. Understandable, considering the state of the cars Doug was pointing at.

"They look like a lot of the cars we passed on our way here. Do they even run?"

A cunning twinkle flared to life in Doug's eyes.

"Looks can be deceiving. I put these babies here for a reason."

He turned to the cars and went on.

"I removed the batteries and the starters and went the extra mile by letting air out of the rear tires."

Steve turned to the five cars and still couldn't believe they were meant to run. He walked closer and tried to look between them, but they were sandwiched pretty tightly.

"How are we even meant to get between them? They seem to be wedged nice and tight."

Doug tapped his nose and smiled.

"Exactly what I was going for. It's meant to look like that, but there's a solution."

Steve paused and turned to his uncle, eager to hear what he had in mind.

"We pull the first one away with the yard's big forklift we passed on the way in. We put the battery and starter back in place, fill up the tires, and repeat the process for the remaining four."

Steve nodded.

"Alright. But how do we get the cars out of here?"

Steve turned and faced the path they followed.

"We can't exactly take them out the way we came. That's more of a walking path."

Doug nodded in agreement.

"I thought about that. Which is why I worked on that fence over there."

Steve stared at the chain fence, looking for a clue as to what Doug was referring to. Doug walked up to the fence and pointed at a sizeable rectangular slot he had welded into the fence.

"It opens and shuts like a door. We will be able to drive the cars out and in without breaking a sweat."

Steve nodded.

"Well, color me surprised. You actually thought this through."

He eyed their surroundings and asked a question.

"So, where did you stash the parts?"

Doug smiled with satisfaction.

"I snuck the starters into the trunk of the station wagon when you weren't looking, and I put the batterers in the trunks of the cars."

Steve stroked his chin.

"That's smart."

Doug clapped Steve on the shoulders and chuckled.

"You'll learn a thing or two if you pay attention. Let me teach you a little something about misdirection."

Steve furrowed his eyebrows.

"Have you been watching those old magic shows again?"

Doug sighed and shook his head.

"No. I was referring to cars. So, they look like they can't drive, and I made sure of that by removing the key parts."

Doug chuckled.

"The best part is that James and all the other scrapyard workers don't suspect a thing."

Doug smiled, proud of what he was able to pull off.

"I told him the engines and transmissions had ceased, and

he took my word for it."

Doug shook his head slowly.

"I almost feel bad. If James had any idea what I was stashing in here, he would be pretty mad."

Steve took a moment to digest all the information provided by his uncle. The more he thought about it, the more impressed he felt.

"How long have you been working on this, exactly?"

Doug shrugged.

"The cars came in one after the other. I just found the ones that were still in working order and stashed them here little by little. It took about eight months, total."

He stared at the sky and sighed.

"It wasn't all smooth sailing. I nearly got caught a couple of times. Thankfully, it all worked out."

Doug grabbed Steve by the shoulders.

"This is just one phase of my master plan."

Doug eyed the cars and was satisfied with what he saw.

"Everything seems to still be in order. Let's get out of here before someone sees us."

Doug and Steve retraced their steps and returned to the station wagon.

⊕

Bo stared at the clock above the counter, eager to get home for the day. He had decided to stop by the grocery store on his way back home and grab some items to go with dinner. The line trailed along and soon it was his turn.

"Good afternoon."

The cashier smiled up at him, and he returned the smile as he handed her his items. The cashier ran the goods over the scanner, and the total flashed up on the small display.

"That will be twenty-six dollars and seventeen cents. Would that be cash or credit?"

Bo produced one of his debit cards and handed it over to the cashier. The jovial lady ran it through the machine and frowned. She tried again, and Bo noticed the look on her face.

"Is something wrong?"

The cashier nodded.

"I'm terribly sorry, but the card was declined."

CHAPTER 5

PUZZLE PIECES

Bo's expression said it all. He could not believe what he was hearing.

"Could it be a machine error? That card should work just fine."

The cashier furrowed her eyebrows as she stared at the screen before her.

"I don't think so, sir. The machine was working fine just a second ago."

Bo ran his fingers through his hair. He produced a second card from his pocket and handed it to the cashier.

"Could you try this one?"

The lady nodded and swiped the card through the machine.

"Alright. We're good to go."

She handed Bo the receipt and smiled as he walked away.

"Have a great day, sir."

He nodded.

"You too. It was probably a bank error. Thank you for your patience."

Bo pushed through the grocery store doors with a confused look on his face.

⊕

Phil peered through the window on Doug's porch before knocking on the door. He waited a moment and spoke up.

"Hey, Doug. Are you home?"

Phil heard Steve yell from the living room.

"It's for you!"

A loud response came from deeper within that Phil was unable to make out. He waited for a couple of seconds, then heard footsteps approaching the door. The door swung open, and Phil found himself staring at the grizzly face of Doug. Doug burped loudly and rubbed his belly as he scowled at Phil.

"Oh, it's you. You wanted to see me?"

Phil nodded and stared at the beer in Doug's clutches.

"Yeah. Do you have a minute to talk, or is this a bad time?"

Doug nodded and stepped aside, holding the door wide open.

"Yeah, I can talk. Let me just finish this beer quickly. Come in."

It wasn't Phil's first time at Doug's place. The musty furniture and dingy interior were as familiar as the stubble on Doug's face. Doug crushed the beer can and tossed it in the yard, missing the nearby garbage can by several feet.

The pair walked into the living room, catching Steve's attention on the entrance. Phil and Steve met eyes for a brief moment. Doug roughly rubbed Steve's hair.

"Scram. The adults need to talk."

Steve shook his head and glared at his uncle.

"Alright, alright. You don't need to be rude about it."

Steve took one more good look at Phil before getting up to leave. Doug collapsed into his easy chair with a loud sigh and stared at Phil, who sat on the couch.

"So, what did you want to talk about?"

Phil twiddled his thumbs and stared off into the distance. It was clear that he was struggling with something. Doug didn't have the patience to wait for him to speak.

"Well?"

Phil sighed heavily and looked up.

"Remember what we talked about at the diner?"

Doug stroked his chin, mockingly considering the question.

"My struggle with sobriety?"

Phil rolled his eyes.

"Haha. You know what I'm talking about."

Phil clenched his fists.

"Since you brought up the old days, that's all I've been able to think about. Doubts that I fought to suppress started to resurface."

Phil averted his eyes and went on.

"Don't get me wrong, I'm not blaming you. It was inevitable. I'd like to hear the rest of what you had to say at the diner."

Doug was courteous enough to keep silent while Phil spoke. He carefully listened to everything his old friend had to say.

"Are you sure? You seemed pretty content with the way things are the last time we talked. How do I know you won't flake out halfway?"

Phil shook his head firmly.

"I'm determined to see this through. You can count on that."

Doug leaned back in his seat and fell silent. He instinctively reached for a beer, but there was none within view. Doug sighed and ran his fingers through his hair as he considered the situation.

"Alright. I trust you know what you're doing."

He leaned in and fixed Phil with a severe stare.

"Listen carefully to everything I'm about to say. You

should know the drill by now. So, I won't repeat myself."

Phil nodded and paid careful attention. Doug took his time to explain his plan to Phil. He went over the various facets and what they entailed. After some time, the pair emerged from Doug's house and walked over to Phil's car. He paused by the car door and turned to Doug.

"So, do you think it'll be easy?"

Doug nodded with confidence.

"Without a doubt."

Phil went on.

"And what about the kid? Do you think he can handle it? I wouldn't want something to go wrong because he fucked up."

Doug held his hand up.

"The kid has been helping me with some of the preparation. I drummed the rules into his head every second I get. He seems competent enough."

That seemed to be enough to satisfy Phil. He still had a question.

"This job, it's pretty large. Are you sure the three of us will be enough?"

Doug furrowed his eyebrows and carefully considered the question.

"If need be, the three of us will be enough. But ideally, we will need a fourth man. I have an idea of the perfect person. It isn't certain whether or not he will join us, though."

Phil paused. The concern on his face was easy to spot.

"Who is this fourth person? Do I know him?"

Doug shook his head.

"I haven't asked him yet."

Doug knew from the past he couldn't say anything just yet. Phil would want him vetted.

Phil faced Doug full-on.

"I'll need some information. Is it reliable? What's his stake in all of this? And most importantly, can we trust him? I don't want any loopholes in this plan."

"Relax. I'm sure we can trust him. You don't know Steve, but you're willing to take my word on his credibility."

Phil shook his head.

"That's different. Steve is your nephew."

Doug walked forward and placed a hand on Phil's shoulder.

"This last guy has a lot more to lose if we botch this up than the rest of us. If he gets involved, you can be sure that he will do his part diligently. I'll tell you anything else you need to know once I'm sure he's in."

Phil didn't look reassured.

"Are you certain this will work?"

Doug stared at the sun in the distance as he responded.

"While I was in the pen, this was all I could think about. I spent hours going over what we did wrong the first time."

He turned to Phil and went on.

"It was a high-class prison, so you had all these guys in for corporate fraud and investment fraud. I made sure to cozy up to them, and I learned the ins and outs."

Phil nodded and sighed.

"I'm actually scared. But that 'what if' brought me here."

Doug nodded understandingly.

"Don't worry. I've been planning this for a very long time. I have all the details worked out. There's nothing left to do but give it a shot."

Phil clenched his fist, and his confidence returned.

"Alright. I'm in, one hundred percent."

Doug smiled from ear to ear and clapped Phil on the back.

"That's what I like to hear. We'll talk soon."

Phil got into his car and drove away. Doug watched him drive off as Steve stepped onto the driveway. He handed Doug a beer.

"I figured you'd need one of these."

Doug smiled at his nephew and grabbed the beer.

"Your mother raised a true gentleman."

He popped open the can and took a large swig.

"So, is he in?"

Doug wiped his mouth and smiled.

"He's in."

Steve looked excited.

"So, the three of us can do it?"

Doug furrowed his eyebrows and stared off into the distance.

"Not quite. I have one more person in mind."

Steve scratched the back of his head.

"Who's that?"

⊕

Bo pulled up to his driveway and the car came to a halt. He stared at his home; his mind plagued by worry. He reached for his phone and dialed before holding it up to his ears. Bo took a deep breath and waited for the ringing to stop. The voice that came through was familiar.

"Hello?"

"Hey. I was calling to ask you something. I was trying to get groceries earlier today, and my card got declined. I thought it was strange, so I talked to my bank, and you won't believe what I found out."

Silence drifted over the line for a brief moment.

"Look, you knew this was going to happen eventually."

Bo clenched his fists and fought to keep the anger out of his voice.

"I know. But I would appreciate it if you told me before taking money from my account in the future."

Bo listened for a brief moment and nodded along with what the banker had to say.

"I know, but..."

He paused again and clenched his jaw. Bo felt a headache coming along and gently massaged his temples as he continued to listen.

"I understand. I'll talk to you later, then."

Bo hung up and tossed his phone into the passenger's seat. He glared for a short while and suddenly slammed his fist into the car horn.

"Shit!"

⊕

The homecoming parade was a big tradition in Steamboat. It was the town's way of praising their local high school football team. The game was scheduled to hold later that afternoon, culminating in a match between their team and their arch-rivals, the Hawks. The city pulled out all the stops and had it all, from parade floats to a full squad of cheerleaders, ready to lead the march. Lined up behind the floats were a mixture of cars, tractors, and other attractions.

The cheerleaders stood in a circle at the front and went over their game plan while waiting for the march to begin. Two ladies in charge of organizing the parade went from group to group, inspecting equipment and making sure everyone knew their order for the parade.

The football players arrived shortly before the march was meant to start, and the organizers approached them.

"We're glad you're here. Are you clear on what to do?"

The team captain nodded to the women and went to work. They helped load some of the bulkier decorations onto the different trucks and vehicles meant to be part of the attraction. Once everything was in place. The team split up into several different vehicles and mounted.

The last piece of the march, and arguably the most important, was the marching band. The band leader had his team assembled to the side and went over a few drills with them. The organizers walked over.

"Is everything ready here?"

The band leader turned to them and smiled.

"You bet. We're excited to begin."

The band leader had his team line up in the proper order and clapped his hands together.

"All ready."

While the parade participants prepared, locals trooped in to get a good view of the procession. The people lined up on either side of the street and craned their necks in anticipation of the march. The parade was something everyone looked forward to seeing. It was a chance to unwind after days of hard work—a chance to relax with family and friends.

After a few minutes of preparation, the procession was ready to begin. The U.S. Army Reserves sent a few delegates to start the parade. The soldiers marched by and held the U.S. and Missouri State flags over their heads. As the flags moved by, the locals got up to pay their respects. Once the flags were through, all eyes turned to the procession behind. It was time for the parade to begin.

It began with the marching band. They played a perfect rendition of "Lady Liberty", setting the entire event's tone and pace. The sound echoed down the street and was closely followed by the first float.

CHAPTER 6

DESPERATE MEASURES

The sound of the marching band could be heard from a reasonable distance away. Many trooped towards the music, eager to witness the parade. Steve watched the people cross the street in front of his car and was on high alert. He checked every angle, waiting for the street to empty so he could make a move.

Several people were late to the festivities, and Steve had to wait for a few minutes before the road emptied. He diverted his attention to Webster's Candy Shop across the street. Steve had been casing out the place for a few days and knew it was the rallying point for the beginning of the parade.

Steve was aware that only one or two employees would be around the building. Not enough to hinder his movements. One employee left with the crowd to see the parade, while the other remained in the back office. Steve checked the time, then grabbed a backpack from the backseat of the car.

From the bag, he pulled out what looked like a bottle of spirits. Steve's hand shook as he eyed the bottle.

"Now isn't the time to pussy out."

He steadied himself and began assembling a Molotov cocktail. Steve stuffed flammable material into the bottle opening and double-checked its security. Once he was confident in his assembly, he grabbed a small light from the bag and stuffed both under his jacket.

Steve looked up from his assembly and eyed the street one more time for good measure. Everyone seemed to be at the parade ground.

"Alright. Let's do this."

Steve grabbed a pair of old BluBlocker shades from the dashboard and put them out. He then got out of the car and hung his head low as he crossed over to the parking lot. A few people walked by once he was out of the car, but they paid him no heed.

Once Steve was on the lot, he made sure to keep the back office within sight while he navigated between the cars. The last thing he needed was for one of the employees to come out at the wrong time.

The majority of the vehicles on the lot were securely locked. Steve tried door after door, but none of them seemed to be open.

"Come on."

Steve knew he needed to be done as quickly as possible. He went up and down the different rows in search of an opportunity. One presented itself in the form of a car with one of the back windows down.

"Score."

Steve watched the back office and crouched as he approached the vehicle. He tried the door handle, but it seemed to be locked.

"Probably left the window down while waiting for the parade to start. This is my lucky day."

Steve stuck his hand through the window and pulled the latch, allowing the door to open up. With the back seat in clear view, Steve produced the cocktail hidden in his jacket and brandished the lighter. He decided to stuff the bottle on the floor of the backseat and set the rag alight.

The rag caught fire quickly, and Steve knew he needed to get out of there. There was some movement in his periphery, and he spotted someone walking past the back-office window. Steve halted, but the door remained shut.

"Time to go."

Steve wiggled his way between the cars and returned to the street. He hopped into his car and drove off.

⊕

Doug and Phil casually walked by the passing floats. A red tractor zoomed past the pair, occasionally halting to hand out candy to kids on the sidewalk. Doug smiled at the sight, and Phil turned to him.

"How can you smile? Aren't you tense?"

Doug slowly shook his head.

"That's a lovely sight. Besides, everything is fine. You should relax."

Phil took a deep breath and steadied his nerves. Another float went by, carrying some of the dignitaries of the parade. The captain of the football team, as well as the king and queen of the parade, were on the float.

Doug watched the float go by, and Phil turned to his watch.

"Where's the kid? He should be here by now."

Doug sighed.

"You really know how to kill the mood. Steve will be here soon. Stop worrying about it and enjoy the parade while you can."

Meanwhile, back at Webster's lot, the Molotov stowed on the floor of the back seat was near bursting. Fire from the cloth trailed up the leather upholstery, setting part of the car on fire before the cocktail itself could ignite. Smoke trailed out of the open back window.

Finally, the windows shattered outward, and flames trailed out of the opening. A high-pitched scream echoed down the street that could be heard in all directions.

⌗

Doug and Phil continued to casually walk up Boyd Street after leaving the parade route. Soon, Steve pulled up to the pair and stopped long enough for them to hop in. Steve pulled away from the sidewalk and continued in the same direction.

"Took you long enough."

Doug spoke up.

"Did you do it?"

Steve nodded calmly.

"I did. I don't think anyone saw me either."

Doug smiled.

"Was the lot empty?"

Steve shook his head slowly.

"There was one guy in the back office, but he never came out. I made sure to lie low just in case."

Doug clapped his nephew on the shoulder.

"That's what I'm talking about! Great work."

He grabbed the duffel bag and riffled through it, handing out rubber gloves and masks. Phil stared at his mask excitedly.

"I'd be lying if I said I wasn't a little hard right now."

Doug shook his head and smiled.

"Keep it together. We haven't even started yet."

He turned to Steve.

"You know where to head, yes?"

Steve nodded and took the next right.

"Alright, we're almost there. Everyone should be clear about their roles. Let's do a quick check. Is everything ready?"

Phil nodded.

"Gloves and masks ready."

Doug zipped down his coat and revealed a bomb strapped

to his chest.

"The star of the show is good to go."

He retrieved a small detonator from the duffel bag and flipped a switch. An indicator light on the vest began to blink furiously, and he smiled.

"Gentlemen, we're in business."

Steve pulled the car to a halt in front of the First Bank of Missouri. The building was large, but not overly so. The outside was painted white, and there was a small set of stairs leading up to the front entrance. Doug stares out the car window and could not spot anyone watching the entrance on the outside.

"Conditions are optimal. Let's head in."

Doug turned to Steve.

"Keep the engine running and be ready to ram the accelerator."

Doug and Phil pulled down their masks and waited for the coast to be clear before stepping out of the car. They ascended the stairs and calmly walked through the door. The bank was a lot emptier than usual. The parade going on had a huge part to play in that. Except for the two cashiers and one customer, Doug and Phil were unable to spot anyone else.

The pair approached the counter, and the cashiers were none the wiser. By the time they realized what was happening, it was too late. Doug pulled open his vest, and Phil pointed a Glock at the customer waiting to be attended to.

"Alright, nobody scream. We wouldn't want something unfortunate to happen, would we?"

The cashiers were shocked into silence. The lady was more surprised than her male counterpart and quickly held up her hands. Phil leveled his weapon at the male cashier.

"The lady over there has the right idea. Hold your hands up and walk out from behind the counter."

Phil hoarded the cashiers out into the open. The other customer was already on his knees.

"Good. Now, lay flat and stay there. As the man said, we don't want to hurt anyone. We'll be in and out before you know it."

Doug pulled up a seat and settled down in front of the hostages.

"This is very simple. You give us the information we need; we get what we came for, and we will be out of your hair. But if anyone makes any sudden moves, " Doug held up the detonator and hovered his finger over the button, "they'll be cleaning you off the walls for weeks. Now, we aren't here for the safe, just the cash registers."

The cashiers were ready to comply. The lady handed the key over to Phil, and he quickly went from register to register. Phil grabbed all the smaller denominations and left the hundreds, as they had already discussed. Once he was sure he had all the money he could handle, he reappeared from around the front desks.

"All clear."

Doug smiled from ear to ear.

"Good. See. That wasn't so hard, was it? Now. We'll get out of your hair."

Doug and Phil backed up and flew out of the exit. Steve was ready and waiting. He put the car in gear and shot out of the driveway just as the pair hopped into the back of the car.

"How did it go?"

Doug maintained his smile.

"All according to plan. We won't have to worry about the cops for some time."

Steve nodded.

"Did you meet a lot of people in there?"

Phil was the one to reply.

"Nope. It was like Doug predicted. There were only two cashiers and one customer."

Steve smiled.

"So, we did it."

Doug's smile dropped.

"Don't get excited just yet. What matters the most is what we do next. You guys are clear on the next step, right? We can't afford any mistakes."

Steve and Phil nodded, and that was enough for Doug. Steve turned onto Boyd Street and continued.

"List off your responsibilities."

Phil rattled his tasks off monotonously.

"I'm meant to handle the equipment and money bags."

Doug turned to Steve, and he spoke.

"I'm coming in this time, and we will switch cars when we come out. Is the second car in place?"

Doug nodded.

"Right where we left it the other day."

"Alright. That should be everything. Remember, time is of the essence. We can't stay in any one spot for too long."

Steve turned into Missouri Route 121 and slowed down as a shopping center drew closer on the left. He took the next turning and parked as close to the shops as possible. The shopping center served as a small pit stop for travelers. It had everything from a small supermarket to Pete's Pizza. Most importantly, it had Eagle's Nest Savings and Loans. Pete's Pizza and E.N.S.L. were a bit more isolated from the rest of the shopping center. E.N.S.L. fit in with the rest of the shopping center. The place was constructed in such a way that customers could drive-through and make quick transactions.

When Doug first described the bank to Phil, the latter had his concerns. He didn't think there would be enough money. But Doug was confident that it would be enough.

Steve cut the engine, and the trio took a moment to catch their breath. Doug eyed the bank closely before speaking up.

"Alright, Phil. The same as last time. Steve, you watch the entrance and let us know if you see anyone approaching. This place is small, so two on the inside should be enough. Steve, you maintain just inside the door keeping a lookout.

Steve nodded in agreement.

"What about the new car?"

"It's on the other side of the bank."

Phil eyed the bank closely.

"You're right about this place being small. Will there be room to isolate the hostages in?"

Doug nodded.

"There should be. If not, we can just make them lie face down on the floor in front of the counter. Same as last time."

Phil focused on preparing his equipment while Doug turned to Steve.

"I'm trusting you to clean up here."

He handed two bottles to Steve and smiled.

"Go crazy."

CHAPTER 7

WILD GOOSE CHASE

Steve grabbed the bottles and stared at them in confusion.

"What do these do again?"

"Ever heard of a bleach bomb?"

Steve slowly shook his head, and Doug sighed.

"Just pour the contents of one bottle into the other and set it down gently on the center armrest. After a few minutes, it will erupt and send bleach flying in all directions."

Steve nodded.

"And we're doing that because?"

"Because we can't afford to leave behind any trace of our presence in this car."

Steve shrugged.

"Why don't we just set a Molotov and burn it to the ground?"

Doug gently shook his head.

"It would draw too much attention to this place. We need to remain unseen and unnoticed for as long as possible. Understood?"

Steve sighed.

"Yeah."

Doug and Phil got out of the vehicle together.

"Good. Hurry it up."

Steve mixed the contents of both bottles and gave it a firm shake for good measure. He stared at the fizz for a second and then placed the bottle on the center console before stepping out of the car. Phil held on to both bags firmly as the trio walked over to the bank. Doug zipped up his jacket mid-way, effectively concealing the bomb as the entrance drew nearer.

⊕

A fire truck rushed up the street and came to a stop in front of Webster's lot. One of the vehicles on the lot was burning uncontrollably and threatened to spread to the surrounding cars. The firefighters acted quickly, drawing out the hose and running over to the problem car.

One of the firemen firmly gripped the head while his partner forced the valve open, allowing a sharp stream of water to race out of the nozzle. The fireman expertly maintained control of the hose and directed the stream of water at the flaming vehicle.

A sizzling sound filled the air as water came into contact with fire, sending steam into the air. The firefighters worked tirelessly to properly put out the fire.

"Luckily, the gas tank hasn't been hit yet. We would be singing a different tune right now if it were."

The other fireman nodded in agreement. It took a few minutes, but the blaze finally died down. The firemen refused to let up and continued to douse the vehicle with fast streams of water.

"Better safe than sorry."

While the firemen fought to keep the flame under control, the sound of sirens filled the air as police cars drove up to Webster's lot. Most of the men that stepped out were in uniforms and helped keep the watching crowd under control. An officer stepped out of a cruiser and gazed at the scene with worry in his eyes.

Andy had been working with the force for quite some time. While vandalism wasn't a rare occurrence, it usually never scaled to this level. He whistled to himself as he approached the lot.

"That's some fire."

Andy, a tall drink of water with light brown hair, housed his hat rather nicely. The color carried over to his facial hair, which helped to properly outline his face. His eyes smiled independently of the rest of his expression, making him look approachable.

Andy was clear about what to do. He needed to question the crowd and figure out if anyone had seen anything. He turned to address the crowd.

"Good morning, folks. Rest assured that the fire is under control. There's no need to panic. If you all could maintain your positions, I would love to ask you some questions." Andy approached a kind but distressed looking lady.

"Good day, ma'am. Are you feeling okay?"

The lady nodded slowly, and he went on.

"How long have you been here?"

"Well, I live across the street, you see. I saw smoke coming from one of the car windows and screamed before rushing off to call it in."

Andy nodded along and scribbled down notes.

"Would you happen to have noticed anyone walking in or out of the lot?"

The lady slowly shook her head.

"I was watching the parade. I'm sorry."

Andy smiled.

"There's no need to apologize. You can go back home now. The fire is under control."

The timid lady nodded and turned to leave. Andy took the

liberty of questioning a few other people before finally pausing to collate what he managed to write down.

"No one saw who walked into that lot. Everyone was busy watching the parade."

Andy tried to wrap his head around the act of vandalism.

"Why would anyone randomly set a car on fire?"

He shrugged and sighed.

"I guess I'll find out soon enough."

Andy returned to the scene of the fire and talked to one of the firemen.

"How's it looking?"

The man frowned and folded his arms.

"The car is destroyed. We're just lucky that it didn't reach the gas tank or any other cars. This entire lot would have been up in flames."

Andy sighed.

"Did you find a cause?"

The fireman shook his head.

"That thing is still scorching hot. We won't be able to search it until it cools."

Andy was about to ask another question when one of the other officers present waved at him. Andy turned and walked off.

"Yeah?"

He held up a receiver.

"Dispatch."

Andy held the receiver to his ear as he spoke.

"This is Andy. Go ahead, dispatch."

"We just received a call about a 211 at the First Bank of Missouri."

Andy assumed he had heard wrong and was quite surprised.

"Sorry, could you say that again?"

"I said a 211 at the First Bank of Missouri. It was just robbed a few minutes ago. One of the cashiers just called it in.

How fast can you get other there?"

The initial shock cleared, and Andy focused. Andy signaled to one of the less busy officers and asked him to follow.

"Whoa. Where are you headed, Andy?"

Andy raced over to his cruiser and hopped into the driver's seat.

"Get in, Frank. We're headed to the First Bank of Missouri."

Frank settled into the passenger's seat with a concerned expression.

"What for?"

Andy put the car in gear and pulled out of the driveway.

"It just got robbed."

⊕

Eagle's Nest Savings and Loans never expected the storm. Doug and Phil ran the same tactic. They took control of people at the bank and got the cashiers to hand over the drawer keys. While Doug watched the hostages with his detonator in hand, Phil proceeded to empty all the registers of all smaller denominations. Once again, he left the hundred-dollar bills alone.

Once Phil was done, Doug rose from his seat and smiled down at the hostages.

"No one got hurt, as I promised. We will be on our way now."

He and Phil backed out of the bank. Steve was keeping watch as they walked out.

Phil and Doug took off their masks, and the latter scanned the area. He smiled when he noticed a car approaching them.

The cruiser stopped in front of them, and Doug wasted no time in boarding.

"Get in! Quickly."

Phil and Steve shared a worried look, but listened to Doug.

Phil opened the back door, and the pair hopped in just before the cruiser shot off. Steve checked over his shoulder, wary of the cops. Phil, on the other hand, focused on the man seated in the driver's seat.

"Who the hell is this, Doug?"

Steve turned and gasped as he noticed who was driving.

"Bo? What the hell are you doing here?"

Bo maintained a straight expression and remained focused on the road.

"What does it look like I'm doing? The car isn't gonna drive itself."

Phil held his hand up.

"Pause. Am I the only one that's lost here? Who is this guy? And why is he driving instead of Steve? This was not part of the plan."

Bo turned in and out of the concrete curbs and drove out of the shopping center's parking lot, making his last left onto Highway 121 heading south.

"I'm Bo. Doug said you needed a fourth man, and it just so happens that I had some free time on my hands."

Bo's sarcasm did not ease Phil's anger. Doug realized he needed to take control of the situation and spoke up before Phil could reply.

"Let's all calm down. Getting agitated won't help anyone. Well, he already told you his name, so I'll just fill in the rest of the blanks."

Doug gestured at Bo.

"Bo here is going to be our getaway driver for the rest of the job. The last two banks were easy pickings, but we will need three men on the inside for this last one. Bo will ensure that the car remains warm so we can get out of there as quickly as possible."

Bo saluted without drawing his eyes away from the road. Phil frowned.

"Where did you get him from? How do we know he can be

trusted?"

Steve interjected.

"I've done some work for Bo in the past. Construction stuff. He's pretty trustworthy."

Bo eased to a halt at the next light, and the sound of sirens cut off the rest of their conversation. Phil checked over the back seat and began to fidget.

"You hear that? The cops are probably on to us."

Doug shook his head.

"Relax. They should probably just be getting to the first bank. Did I remember to tell the teller to count to a hundred before calling? It doesn't matter, anyway."

Phil shook his head.

"Sounds like it matters to me. We need to end this quickly."

Doug nodded in agreement.

"We're all on the same page. So, how about we stop questioning each other and focus on the job?"

After sitting at a stoplight, the crew proceeded onward to their next destination. Bo eyed the next turning and gently eased into a smaller strip mall before drawing the car to a halt. He looked over his shoulder.

"Alright, the stuff Doug asked for is in the back."

Phil reached over the back seat and retrieved another green duffel bag. He opened it up, revealing masks and gloves.

"We already have these."

Doug shook his head.

"No, we need to change them. It'll throw the cops off the scent a little."

Phil nodded and grabbed the new masks as Doug turned to Bo.

"Did you get every single thing on that list?"

Bo took a moment to mentally check off the list, then nodded. Doug sighed.

"That's good. Alright, we need to dispose of the old equipment. Dump all your masks and gloves into this trash bag."

Doug produced a sizeable bag and dumped his gloves and masks before handing it over to Steve. Steve and Phil did as they were asked, and Doug spoke up.

"There should be bleach and glow sticks somewhere in that duffel bag. Dump the stuff into the trash bag and toss it into the bin."

Steve stared at the glow sticks in confusion.

"What am I meant to do with these?"

"Rip them open and dump the contents into the bag. It'll help the bleach dissolve any traces of us faster. Do it just outside the car. We wouldn't want to get any of that stuff on ourselves."

Steve stepped out of the car and went about dumping chemicals into the trash bag. The smell was pretty nauseating, but he managed to pull through.

"All done."

Doug smiled.

"Good. Now, toss it and get back in here."

Steve found a bin not too far from where they parked and tossed the trash bag in. He returned to the vehicle just as Bo drove off again. Bo navigated through the strip mall and got to the back, just at the edge of a hill. Doug looked down and smiled.

"Would you look at that? You can see the second bank from here."

Phil peered through his window and nodded.

"It doesn't look like there are any cops there."

Doug nodded.

"By the time they get here, we will be long gone."

CHAPTER 8

LURKING THREAT

Andy and Frank were the first to arrive on the scene. The bank looked peaceful on the outside, but the second they walked through the door, it was chaos. The cashier and teller were pacing back and forth while arguing with one another. There seemed to be one more person present, and he was in so much shock that he sat silently in the corner. The teller looked up at their arrival and sighed with exhaustion.

"Glad you could finally make it."

The teller was middle-aged, with graying hair and a stocky build. She ambled over to the officers as they approached and frantically began to speak while trying to express herself. Andy held out his hands.

"I'm going to need you to calm down, ma'am. Take a deep breath."

The lady listened to Andy and took long, deep breaths. She calmed down considerably, and Andy smiled.

"Everything is going to be just fine. Why don't you say that again? Slowly this time."

The teller nodded and spoke up.

"I was afraid they would come back. Thank you for coming."

Andy nodded.

"Could you run me through what happened here? And feel free to be as detailed as possible."

The male cashier, who was a lot younger than the lady, walked over to join them.

"Is everything alright here?"

The lady nodded.

"I was just about to tell the officer what happened. Could you help fill in the blanks? It happened so fast."

The cashier nodded as the lady began her tale.

"It wasn't long after the parade started. Nicholas and I were attending to a customer, Chester, over there, when these thugs burst in. Oh, my."

Nicholas placed a calming hand on the lady's shoulder, and she went on.

"They demanded that we get out from behind the counter and drop to the floor."

Andy took notes as he listened.

"Did they hold you at gunpoint?"

Nicholas nodded.

"One of them did. The other had a bomb strapped to his chest."

Andy paused with his pen poised over the notepad.

"A bomb?"

The lady nodded.

"I could tell because I've seen a couple on TV. It was horrifying to look at."

Andy furrowed his eyebrows, concerned about the news he was hearing.

"Are any of you hurt? Do I need to call an ambulance?"

Nicholas shook his head.

"We didn't resist, so they weren't violent. They just took the money and left."

Andy noted that and paused.

"Did you take note of how much they took?"

The lady shook her head.

"Honestly, I was too scared to keep my eyes open."

Andy nodded.

"That's understandable. And you haven't been into the drawers since they left?"

Nicholas nodded.

"We didn't want to risk angering them in case they decided to come back. We stayed on the ground for a little while, and when we finally worked the nerve to get up, we called you right away. We've been anxiously waiting since then."

While Andy continued to question the cashier, Frank checked up on the customer.

"Are you alright down there?"

Chester looked up and smiled weakly.

"Yeah, just a little shaken up. It's not every day you witness something like that. It really gets the blood pumping."

Frank nodded.

"Are you hurt? Want me to ring up the paramedics?"

Chester shook his head and got up from his sitting position.

"Fit as a fiddle. Thanks for the concern. It's a shame what happened, though. The First Bank of Missouri has always been here. This robbery affects all of us."

Frank agreed.

"Hopefully, we can catch the sons of bitches that did this before they spend any of the cash."

Frank eyed the banking hall, searching for any clues that would lead to the culprits.

"Will you be fine on your own? I'd like to do a little investigating."

Chester nodded.

"Go ahead. I'll be fine."

Frank patted him on the shoulder and stalked off. He

walked to the other side of the counter and took note of all the destruction and chaos. Tellers had been tossed to the floor, and the area was in disarray. Frank whistled softly.

"They really did a number here."

Frank carefully threaded over the fallen items and kept his eyes peeled on essential areas. All the drawers had been emptied. Frank noticed some bills on the floor and walked standing over them.

"I better wear gloves beyond this point."

He was smart enough to avoid tampering with potential evidence during his investigation. Frank carefully held the register door open and peered into the back. Aside from money, there seemed to be no other valuables missing.

Frank heard Andy approaching behind him, but kept examining the safe for clues.

"So, what do you think?"

Frank looked up and came eye to eye with his partner.

"Standard mess behind the counter. They were thorough in their search."

Andy nodded.

"My thoughts exactly. What exactly did they take?"

Frank walked forward and scanned the shelves.

"Only the money trays were targeted."

Andy walked up to one of the trays and noticed that a few bills were remaining.

"They missed a few, it seems."

Frank turned with a start.

"Are you sure?"

Andy nodded and gestured at the bin in front of him. Frank walked over to check it out and scratched his head in confusion.

"That makes no sense. These guys were careful enough to get back here. I don't think they would have overlooked any of the money."

Andy put on latex gloves and reached for a collection of

bills.

"These are the high denominations, too."

Frank slowly shook his head.

"Something doesn't add up. What do you think?"

Andy stared at the hundred-dollar bills in his hand and slowly shook his head.

"I have a bad feeling about this."

⌗

Bo made a U-turn and traveled down the hill. Phil continued to stare at Eagle's Nest until the shopping complex vanished completely. Once at the foot of the hill, the group lost sight of Miller Road. Bo pointed to a string of buildings across the street.

"Is it there?"

Doug nodded and smiled.

"That's the place. Floor it."

Bo did as he was told and rammed down the gas. He drifted onto a closed-off street and parked out of view of the main road. Doug eyed the buildings surrounding them, and his gaze locked onto a convenience store within walking distance.

"The last car is in the alleyway next to that shop. You guys know the drill."

Doug produced a trash bag and handed it to the guys at the back.

"Nothing remains in here. Clear the vehicle."

Phil and Steve made sure that all traces of them went into the trash bag. Once that was done, Steve held the back up to Doug.

"You too."

Doug cleared the passenger seat and held onto the trash bag. Bo kept his eyes peeled on the convenience store while they worked.

"There doesn't seem to be a lot of activity on this road. I'll go get the last car. You guys wait here."

Bo checked up and down the street one more time before stepping out of the car. He casually walked up to the convenience store and disappeared down the alley next to it. Phil watched Bo trudge off with a glare.

"I still don't trust him."

Phil turned on Doug with a cold stare and went on.

"You told me you would let me know the second he was confirmed. I don't appreciate the lapse in communication."

Doug shrugged.

"I wasn't sure he would come, not until I saw him pull up in front of that bank. And boy, am I glad he came."

Phil palmed his face and sighed.

"You're not one to leave things hanging in the air like that. How can I trust someone I just met? For all I know, he is going to head straight to the cops as soon as we split up."

Doug shook his head firmly.

"Bo wouldn't do that. He stands to lose a lot more if this deal goes south. Bo isn't like us; he doesn't have any priors. He is generally well-liked, and he has a business to boot. Imagine what would happen to his credibility if he were caught helping with a crime like this? Bo would lose all his clients, and his business will go down under. If that isn't enough incentive for you to trust him, I don't know what is."

Phil took a deep breath and considered all the facts Doug put forward.

"I still have no idea what his role in this group is exactly."

Doug gently massaged the bridge of his nose with his thumb and forefinger.

"You're giving me a headache. He is the getaway driver. Plain and simple. We need a three-man team on the inside; the next bank is quite large."

Phil nodded.

"Then he'll only get driver money. Because, quite frankly,

I wasn't planning on sharing the loot four ways."

Doug held up his hand.

"Don't you worry about that! There will be more than enough to go around."

Doug turned to Steve.

"You've been awfully quiet, boy. What do you think?"

Steve shrugged.

"Bo is a good guy. I trust your judgment. I kind of understand where Phil is coming from, though. He doesn't know Bo as well as me."

Phil harrumphed and folded his arms.

"Whatever. But if he is getting an equal cut, he will go down with the rest of us if this goes south."

Doug shook his head slowly.

"You're overthinking things. I'm the one with a bomb strapped to my chest. The rest of you will get off lightly. But I don't believe it will come to that. As long as we stick to the plan. Capisce?"

Doug's attention was drawn to the alley beside the convenience store as a car pulled out of the shadows. The car drove down the street and made a U-turn before coming to a halt behind the trio.

"Our new ride is here. Let's get on with it."

Bo walked up to the window and addressed Steve.

"The chemicals needed for the bleach bomb are deep within the duffel bag in see-through containers. It would be hard to miss them. I also got what you need to fill the trash bag."

Steve produced the chemicals and nodded as he got to work. The rest carried all they needed from one car to the other. Steve was careful to fill the bag with bleach. He tied it up and tossed it into the trash can before returning to the car.

"Right. Now, the car."

Doug produced both bottles needed to create the bleach bomb and carefully poured the contents of one into the other.

He shook the container for good measure and placed it on the center console. The other three were in the new car, with the engine running as he hopped in.

"Did you handle the trash bag as I instructed?"

Doug nodded his head.

"I only handled it with gloves on like you said, and made sure the bleach was everywhere."

Doug smiled and nodded.

"And the car?"

Doug eyed the vehicle warily.

"The bleach bomb is sitting and waiting. I wouldn't want to be here when that thing goes off."

Bo nodded in agreement.

"Good point. Are we good to go?"

Doug mentally dotted his I's and crossed his T's.

"I think we are. Let's go."

Bo put the car in gear and drove out of the closed road. He double-checked both sides to ensure they were clear and faced them toward Miller Road. The car was eerily silent for the duration of the ride. Tensions were high. Everyone realized it all came down to the last one.

They were terrified and excited at the same time.

CHAPTER 9

TWO FRONTS

Heidi enjoyed her job. She enjoyed helping people get the help they needed. While Steamboat rarely had large incidents, small calls came in every once in a while. That day was an exception. Heidi was genuinely surprised to hear about the robbery.

"You don't see that every day. I hope they get there on time."

She pulled up her magazine and went back to reading about her favorite celebrities. She enjoyed getting lost in their luxurious lives and focused all her attention on her reading. Ten minutes later, the phone rang, drawing Heidi back to the present.

She put down her magazine and picked up the phone.

"Hello, 911. What's your emergency?"

Heidi patiently listened to what the caller had to say and penned it down.

"A robbery, you say? Calm down, Miss. The police are on their way."

Heidi initially assumed it to be a double call. Sometimes,

different people called to report the same thing. She hung up the phone and stared at the receiver.

"I should probably check in with the unit I called."

Heidi dialed and was soon put through to an officer.

"Are you at the bank yet?"

"Yeah, we got here a few minutes ago."

Heidi furrowed her eyebrows as she considered the situation.

She figured there was a mix up somewhere but didn't know how to proceed.

"Well, as long as they are on the ground. Everything else should fall into place."

Heidi was about to pick up her magazine when the phone rang again.

"Hello, 911. What is your emergency?"

Again, the caller reported a robbery.

"Relax, Miss. Where are you right now?"

The location surprised her, and she penned it down.

"The police will arrive shortly. Please, hold on."

Heidi replaced the phone and stared at the receiver.

"Two different robberies on the same day. Who would have thought?"

Once again, she picked up the receiver and dialed.

⊕

Andy and Frank emerged from the safe while conversing with one another.

"Let's try gathering a little more information before we move on."

Andy returned to the teller and talked her up.

"Were you able to make out any of the attackers? Did you notice a face by chance or any discernable features?"

The lady thought for a moment before responding.

"The man with the bomb strapped to his chest sounded

rather pleasant. It's hard to describe his voice. They wore masks and kept their faces covered throughout."

Andy sighed and slowly shook his head.

"I was afraid of that. If you remember anything at all. Please, don't hesitate to call the station. Any information will be considered helpful."

The communicator on Andy's shoulder buzzed to life, and a voice came through.

"Are you at the bank yet?"

Andy nodded to no one in particular.

"Yeah. We got here a few minutes ago."

Andy paused for a moment and resumed his questioning.

"So, about the situation during the robbery. It was just both of you behind the counter, correct?"

The teller nodded.

"Is that normal? To only have two employees present."

The lady shook her head slowly.

"There are meant to be three or more employees on the ground at any given time. But today was an exception because of the parade."

Andy raised a single eyebrow.

"Who was meant to be here with the two of you?"

"The office manager. He came in and left early to see the parade. His son is on the football team."

Andy was forming a narrative in his mind, but he needed more details.

"Who knew you would be shorthanded today? I doubt that's something that would be publicly announced."

The teller nodded.

"We talked about it yesterday evening before closing for the day. Honestly, aside from us three and maybe the manager, I don't think anyone else should have known."

Andy found that interesting. The fact that the bank was attacked on the day they were shorthanded couldn't have been a coincidence.

"Has the office manager returned?"

The teller searched the banking hall and shook her head.

"I haven't seen him since he left this morning."

Andy furrowed his eyebrows as he filed away that bit of information.

"I see. Have you tried calling him?"

The lady shook her head.

"Honestly, I forgot until you asked right now. The only thing I could think of when the robbers left was calling you guys."

Andy turned to the cashier.

"How about you, Nicholas? You've been awfully quiet."

Nicholas sighed and nodded.

"Sorry, it's just hard to calm down after such a terrifying experience. As she said, I haven't heard from the office manager all morning. I saw him leave early this morning and waved goodbye. Nothing since then. And like she said, the only thing I could think about after the robbery was getting through to you guys."

Andy found it a little strange that the office manager was missing. The fire at the parking lot should have at least made him question his absence from work.

"Okay, then. I need to talk to him and get his side of the story. Please, tell him to reach out to me down at the police station the second he returns. It is important."

Nicholas nodded, and in the same breath, Andy heard static from his communicator.

"This is dispatch."

Andy lifted his walkie-talkie slightly and responded.

"This is Andy, go ahead."

"Andy, the teller called again and asked when you would be arriving."

Andy stared at his communicator with a confused expression.

"Are you sure about that, dispatch? I'm standing next to

the teller right now."

Static drifted through for some time before a voice replied.

"I just got off of the phone with her a couple of seconds ago. She says she can't spot neither heads nor tails of you."

Andy turned to the teller and spoke up.

"Is there anyone else here? Another teller I don't know about?"

The lady frowned and shook her head.

"As I said, we are the only tellers on duty. Is something wrong?"

Heidi spoke up.

"Andy, what bank are you at currently?"

Andy picked up his receiver and spoke.

"First Bank of Missouri. Why?"

"That explains it. This lady is calling from Eagle's Nest Savings and Loans. The one at the shopping complex in Jefferson Square."

Andy walked forward.

"Wait, what? But when you called a couple of minutes ago, this was the place you mentioned."

"I know. There were two different callers. I'm sorry it took me so long to clear up the confusion."

Andy paused mid-stride and stared forward in utter shock.

"Wait, so another bank was robbed?"

Frank heard his partner from across the hall.

"Did I hear that, right?"

He got up and trudged over to Andy's side, waiting for a response.

"Looks like it. Get there as fast as you can."

⊕

While the police were in disarray, Doug and his accomplices pulled up to the entrance of Boatman's Bank. They all stared at the entrance with solemn expressions. Everyone understood the gravity of the situation.

"It all comes down to this," said Phil, as he took a deep breath. Doug thought it fit to say a short speech.

"He's right. It all boils down to this, the last job. Keep your heads in the game and remember to remain calm. If we screw up here, it could be the end."

The others silently nodded, and Doug took a deep breath.

"Good. Let's do it."

Doug opened his door slightly and stayed low, peering through the open window. Phil and Steve did the same.

"The three of us are headed in. You all remember your roles, I believe."

Steve and Phil nodded in confirmation, and Doug turned to Bo.

"You will stay in the car and watch the entrance."

Doug fished inside his bag and handed Phil a walkie-talkie.

"If you see anything even slightly suspicious, give us a heads up."

Bo nodded and eyed the road around them.

"I'll do a U-turn and park facing the opposite direction. That way, we don't lose any time trying to get away." ·

Doug liked the sound of that.

"I'll also leave the back door slightly open, so you can just dive in the second you get back."

Phil smiled.

"It looks like the newcomer is earning his cut; way to think on your toes. All three of us will just dive into the back. We can think about comfort when we're home free."

Doug nodded slowly.

"That's actually a great idea. Don't forget to keep the engine running."

Bo flashed him a thumbs up, and Doug turned his attention to the bank. He took a deep breath and zipped up his coat halfway.

"Masks on. Let's move."

Doug, Phil, and Steve put their masks on and made a break for the bank together. Doug told them to pause at the entrance and peeked through the glass divider. Once he was sure that the coast was clear, he spoke up.

"Here goes nothing."

The trio burst into the bank, with Doug leading the charge.

⊕

Andy and Frank stood around the entryway with their jaws almost grazing the floor. The teller overheard what Heidi said and slowly shook her head.

"That isn't us. Maybe it's a different set of robbers."

On a hunch, Andy spoke into the communicator.

"Dispatch, this is Andy again. Did the caller mention how many people were on the scene?"

Silence followed for a brief second as Heidi sourced for the needed information.

"She did. She said three men came in suddenly and left. No further details were offered."

The teller's eyes doubled in size.

"That's not the same number of people that robbed us."

Andy ran his fingers through his hair and frowned.

"I'm going to check things out at Eagle's Nest."

Andy stalked off towards the exit, and Frank followed.

"I'll come with you."

Andy paused and held his hand up.

"No. You stay here and finish up. Make sure you get as much information from this trio as possible. You know how important that is."

Frank stopped and nodded.

"You can count on me."

Andy sighed, relieved to hear that. He pushed through the bank doors and made a beeline for his police cruiser. He grabbed his gun and settled into his seat.

He put on the police siren and gunned down the street at top speed. Andy had a lot of information to sift through in his head. Still, he decided to focus on getting to his destination.

"I need to get to the bottom of this."

⌗

Phil, Doug, and Steve walked into the bank like they owned the place. Only the cashiers looked up at their entrance, leaving the two customers unaware.

"You know what to do."

Doug unzipped his vest, revealing the bomb, and the cashiers cowered in fear. Steve seized the opportunity and dashed behind the counter. He crowded the pair to the front.

"Move it! On the floor, now!"

Phil firmly grasped his weapon and carefully searched the rest of the building. He spotted a lady working behind the glass at the bank and tapped on the divider. Phil pointed his weapon at her, causing her to raise her hands.

"Get out."

The lady did as she was told and walked out from behind the glass. Phil herded her to the front and took control of the situation.

"Everyone, on the ground."

The women whimpered as they dropped to their knees. The men glared at the trio, but Doug ignored them.

"Is that everyone?"

Phil nodded.

"I only found one person in the back. Everyone should be gathered in this room."

There were two women and three men, including the customers. While it was a little more than Doug had estimated, it was still within reason.

"Good. Then we can begin."

CHAPTER 10

CLOSE CALL

Doug paced in front of the hostages as he spoke.

"Sorry to interrupt your day. If you cooperate with us, we will be out of your hair before you know it."

He paused mid-stride and leaned in closer to the hostages.

"But if any of you try something heroic," Doug brought the bomb detonator closer and swung his thumb around the button,

"Well, that would be unfortunate."

Phil took over once Doug was done.

"Now, which of you has the key to the registers? Be snappy about it. I don't like to repeat myself."

The ladies cowered in fear while the men maintained their defiant glares. The lady Phil had retrieved from the back room held her hand up. Phil walked over to her.

"Hand it over."

The teller reached for her hand and removed a bracelet. She handed it over to Phil and dropped her hands, content to quietly whimper while staring at the floor. Phil stared at the bracelet and smiled. He signaled Steve to follow him, and the pair made their way behind the counter.

"Right, while they work on that. What say we have a little chat."

Doug leaned closer and dropped his volume a bit.

"There's a vault at the back, and I want into it. So, which of you has the key combination?"

No one immediately offered a response, and that agitated Doug.

"I've been cordial since we got here, but I will be rough if it is necessary. Who has the fucking key combination?"

The ladies inched away from Doug. The male teller responded.

"None of us have the combination. You can't get into it."

Doug smiled under his mask, and his tone turned icy.

"And you expect me to believe that? One of you has to have it."

The teller sighed and shook his head.

"A new off-site security system was recently put in place. It completely locks down the vault over the weekend."

Doug was genuinely surprised to hear that. He had not factored that possibility into his calculations. Phil overheard their conversation and spoke up.

"That sounds like a load of bull to me."

Doug held up his hand.

"Don't worry, I've got this."

Doug took a deep breath before responding.

"Alright, you have one minute to explain. Go."

The teller nodded and spoke up.

"The bank recently beefed up security. One of the changes that was made was to put a security company in charge of the vault. They decide who gets access inside the vault and completely seal it off on weekends."

Doug heard Steve and Phil working on the registers in the background and nodded along to what the teller said. He digested all the information handed to him by the teller and spoke up.

"So, there is no way into the vault?"

The man nodded.

"No keypad, no lock, nothing. The vault door is remotely controlled."

Doug massaged the bridge of his nose and thought carefully.

"How do you get money when the registers are low?"

The teller fell silent, and one of the ladies took over. The teller was middle-aged but looked surprisingly young for her age. She had streaks of gray in her brown hair, and her brown eyes were safely hidden behind a pair of horn-rimmed glasses. The lady adjusted her glasses before responding.

"We get permission to go into the vault and stock up a smaller safe behind the counter."

Phil overheard and searched for a safe once he and Steve were done emptying the registers. He couldn't spot any traditional-looking safe.

"There's nothing here."

The lady shook her head slowly.

"The bottom cabinet on the far left."

Phil opened the cabinet door and tucked comfortably into the compartment was safe. Phil whistled and leaned in closer.

"It's a standard combination lock."

Doug nodded and addressed the lady.

"You're doing great so far. So, what's the code?"

The lady fell silent. Doug noticed some hesitation in her eyes and slowly shook his head.

"Look, lady. We just want to get the cash and leave. Don't make this more difficult than it must be."

He leaned in close and continued.

"What's the code?"

The lady whimpered and looked away. A younger teller filled in the blanks, a brunette in her early twenties. She placed a calming hand on the middle-aged lady's shoulder, and that helped calm her down.

"I-it's on the key strap I gave the other guy. On the inner band."

Phil flipped the band over and stared at the numbers written on it.

"Got it."

Doug smiled, and his tone lightened.

"See, that wasn't so bad, was it?"

The lady kept her eyes fixed on the floor as she shook her head. Phil immediately went to work. He kept the band under an intense light to correctly see the numbers as he dialed them in. He took his time to make sure each thimble in the safe lock properly clicked, and it seemed to drag out. Doug stared at his watch and paced back and forth as he waited for the safe to be cracked upon.

"We need to be under two minutes guys!"

Phil didn't allow Doug's warning to faze him and soon cracked the last thimble.

"Got it!"

Doug sighed and settled down considerably.

"Good. Remember, only take the small stuff. No Benjamin's. Just fifties and down."

Phil looked at the money in the safe and frowned.

"I don't know. There's a ton of cash in here."

Doug walked closer to the counter.

"Stick to the plan. Need I remind you what happens when someone messes up?"

Phil frowned and slowly shook his head.

"Good. Hurry it up."

While Phil was the one that spoke up, it was clear that Steve didn't like the sound of Doug's warning either. He stared bitterly at the hundred-dollar bills, and Phil clapped his shoulder.

"Don't worry about it. Let's just grab what we can."

Steve handed stacks of bills over to Phil, and the latter

loaded them into a bag. They developed a steady rhythm and managed to get a lot done in a short amount of time. Soon, the safe was nearly empty, except for a few hundred-dollar bill stacks, and Phil rose to his feet.

"Alright, that's all of it. We're good to go."

He picked up one of the bags and was ready to leave, but Steve remained crouched in front of the safe and continued to stare at the hundreds. Phil eyed Steve over his shoulder and yelled.

"Let's go. We don't have time for this."

Phil walked out from behind the counter, and Steve continued to eye the bills. He picked up one collection and quickly leafed through it with his thumb. Steve was plagued with uncertainty but finally decided on what to do. He shoved the cash down the front of his pants and grabbed the sack before walking out from behind the counter.

Doug and Phil were talking while they waited for Steve to finish.

"Any word from the guy outside?"

Doug slowly shook his head.

"Nothing yet."

As he completed his sentence, a vehicle just pulled into the center drive-through of the bank.

Phil and Doug eyed each other, and both looked at each other. They noticed a truck parked in the drive-through lane and quickly dropped below the window. Phil spoke up.

"Oh crap, there's someone there."

Steve immediately noticed something was wrong and dropped down behind the counters. Doug peered over the windowsill and noticed that the older man driving the truck wasn't looking in their direction.

"He's not looking yet."

He turned to Steve and frowned.

"Stay low and get over here quickly."

Steve did as he was told. Phil hobbled over to the entrance, and Steve joined him there while Doug kept watching on the new arrival. Phil sighed.

"What do we do now?"

Doug remained confident and did not panic even slightly.

"Relax. We'll get out here soon. We're going to lie low and get to the car as fast as we can on my signal."

Steve was clearly puzzled. He gazed up at the window above Doug and was about to ask a question.

"But, what if..."

Doug cut him off with a glare.

"Do as I say if you want to get out of here alive."

Phil sighed, and Steve nodded. Doug hobbled over to his partners and stayed crouched beside them.

"Remember to wait for my signal."

He turned to the hostages and smiled.

"Thank you for your time. Thanks to your cooperation, no one got hurt. We will be leaving now, but stay on the floor and count to a hundred. You can move after that, understood?"

The hostages nodded, and that seemed to satisfy Doug.

"Very good."

Doug double-checked the other window and nodded to himself when he noticed it was still empty.

"The old man isn't coming out. Now's our chance. We move out on three."

Doug held his hand against the door and began his count.

"One, two, three."

He pushed through the door first, followed closely by Steve and Phil. The trio made their way over to the parked vehicle at the bottom of the steps while ensuring to remain low. As Bo had promised, the car was facing the opposite direction, and the back door was wide open. Bo watched as they rushed through the back door and shut it firmly. A horn sound came from the drive-through.

"What was that all about?"

Doug eyed the bank and did not explain. He, Phil, and

Steve removed their masks and stuffed them back into the duffel bag before scrunching down in the back seat.

"Just go!"

Bo put the car in gear and floored it. The vehicle screeched away and turned the corner. Bo expertly maneuvered down and around the side entryway and drove behind the bank. The rear entrance was a steep hill that placed them right on Highway 121.

While he drove, Doug and Steve kept watch of their rear while Phil muttered to himself incoherently. The entire group was on edge, but they all calmed down once they were on the highway.

"What the hell happened in there? Did someone show up; was there any trouble?"

Doug took a deep breath and calmed down.

"No. He drove up and stayed in his truck; never came out."

Bo furrowed his eyebrows.

"Do you think he saw any of you?"

Phil kept staring through the windows. He eventually relaxed when he realized they weren't being followed.

"I have no idea. He just parked and sat there. He didn't even roll down his window."

Steve frowned.

"Do you think he could identify us?"

Doug stroked his chin and thought of the scenario they had managed to escape.

"I don't think so. He was in the drive-through but didn't get out. There's not much he could see from there. Plus, we had masks on."

Bo kept his eyes peeled on the road the entire time.

"I don't hear any sirens."

Phil nodded.

"I think we're in the clear."

Doug got up slightly and eyed the road around them. He

didn't spot a single cop car and nodded in agreement.

"I think we can get up now. This place is small enough as it is without us squishing each other."

CHAPTER 11

THE COVER-UP

Andy's car barreled down the street with his siren blaring at a high pitch. He pulled into the shopping complex and parked in front of Eagle's Nest Savings and Loans. A lady frantically paced back and forth in front of the bank and looked up at his arrival. Andy jogged forward and paused by the distressed lady.

"Are you the one that called in a robbery?"

She stifled a sob and nodded.

"Where have you been? I called a long time ago."

Andy could tell that he was in for it.

"Sorry, it took so long for me to arrive. There was a small mix up on the bank locations. The First Bank of Missouri also got robbed."

Andy gave the lady a once over.

"Are you hurt?"

The lady shook her head.

"No, thankfully. Three men barged in, and one of them had a bomb on his chest. It was scary."

Andy could not believe what he was hearing. The narrative

matched what happened at the First Bank of Missouri.

"Is anyone in there hurt? Do I need to call an ambulance?"

The lady slowly shook her head.

"No. They just took the money and left. No one was hurt."

Andy patted the lady on her shoulder and tried his best to calm her down.

"Everything is alright now. I'm here. Why don't we go inside and talk about what happened? I'll need as much detail as possible."

The teller took a deep breath and stopped herself from crying. She forced a brave stare and turned to lead the way. Andy was at the door when static came through his communicator.

"This is dispatch."

Andy drew the walkie-talkie closer.

"Yeah. I just arrived at Eagle's Nest. Everything should be fine now."

Heidi replied.

"I wish that were the case. I just got a call from Boatman's Bank on Miller."

Andy did not like where the conversation was headed.

"Don't tell me..."

Heidi confirmed his fears.

"It was just robbed."

Andy walked over to a chair within the bank and took a seat. His face was a picture of confusion and worry.

"What?"

⊕

Once Boatman's Bank was out of view, the rest of the ride was smooth sailing. Doug could have sworn he heard a siren in the distance, but the sound eventually died down.

"Looks like we're home free."

Bo continued down the highway as they had planned.

"So, what now?"

Doug leaned back in his seat and allowed himself a brief moment of satisfaction.

"Now, we dispose of the evidence."

He turned to Bo and continued.

"James and Junk. Do you know it?"

Bo furrowed his eyebrows as he considered the question.

"Yeah. I know it. Want me to head there?"

Doug nodded.

"The other cars are effectively useless with the bleach bombs in place, but in addition to bleaching this one, I would also like to scrap it. Just to be on the safe side. Most of the guys down at the scrapyard will be at the parade, so we will have enough privacy to get all of this done and go over our next move."

Bo nodded.

"Alright, then."

Continuing south on 121, Bo drove across the county line taking them on the long way around. The drive only lasted for a few minutes, but it felt like hours. Eventually, James and Junk came into view, and Bo paused a good distance away from it.

"So, do we go through the front entrance?"

Doug slowly shook his head.

"I don't want to risk running into someone watching the gates. Take her around back."

Bo put the car in gear and drove around back. He circled the fence until Doug told him to stop.

"Right there."

Doug pointed to a break in the fence and got out of the car. He opened up the entrance he had built, and Bo was able to drive in. Doug checked all the corners to make sure no one was watching and carefully shut the gate behind him.

Everyone got out of the car, and Doug took charge.

"First things first, we need to get out of these clothes.

Everyone prepared spares as I asked?"

They all nodded, and Doug smiled.

"Then get to it."

Doug grabbed some threads from the trunk of a car parked not too far from them and changed. Soon, they all converged by the trunk of their getaway car. Doug looked at every one of his associates in the eyes and spoke.

"Alright, gentlemen. We don't have much time."

He popped open the trunk of the getaway car and revealed two duffle bags. One filled to the brim with money, the other zipped up.

"There it is. The fruit of our labor."

He looked up.

"Is everyone clear about what to do?"

Steve nodded and spoke up.

"Get the loader."

Phil was next.

"I need to pull the plates on this car and grab all the remaining trash bags."

Doug interjected.

"Have you all loaded up the clothes?"

They all nodded, and Doug smiled.

"Good."

He turned to Bo.

"And you?"

Bo folded his arms as he responded.

"Transport the money to a safe location for counting."

Phil frowned.

"I don't think I'm comfortable with that. Why does he get to count the money?"

Doug held his hand up.

"Because that's part of the plan."

Phil shook his head and paced back and forth. He kept his eyes fixed on his feet and muttered to himself as he did so. Doug and Bo remained calm the entire time, and Steve looked more uncomfortable than worried. He adjusted his pants and waited for Phil to say something.

"No deal. I'm not letting this money out of my sight."

Doug rolled his eyes.

"Why don't you speak up a bit? I don't think you were loud enough for the cops to hear."

Steve turned from his uncle to Phil with a worried expression.

"What's the problem."

Phil glared at Bo and approached him menacingly. He stabbed his finger into Bo's chest as he spoke.

"He's the problem. First, Doug didn't tell me there would be the fourth man until the fourth man showed up. Which makes me question his trust in me."

Doug shook his head.

"As I said, I didn't know myself till he showed up."

Phil nodded.

"That's all well and fine. But now, you expect me to trust someone I just met a couple of minutes ago with the most important task in this job? See things from my perspective."

Bo furrowed his eyebrows.

"I thought I earned your trust during the job. You seemed impressed with my driving."

Phil shook his head.

"That doesn't automatically make us best pals."

Doug felt a headache coming along. He gently massaged his temples as he tried to focus.

"You're making this more complicated than it needs to be. Bo has done nothing to earn this much distrust from you."

Bo held up his hand.

"It's alright."

He calmly walked up to Phil and surprised him with a smile.

"Phil, was it? Look, I understand where you're coming from. You wouldn't want to leave something so important to an unknown factor."

Phil nodded slowly.

"Look, Doug reached out to me the same way he reached out to you. We all have a reason to be here, and we all worked hard to make this a success. You may not know me very well, but I have no reason to cheat anyone."

Bo pointed at the bag of money and went on.

"There's enough in there for all of us to walk out of here with our fair shares and be satisfied. Why would I deprive you of that?"

Doug noticed Phil wavering slightly, and so did Bo. Bo placed a hand on Phil's shoulder and continued.

"We worked on this together. We're partners now until all of this blows over. What say we bury the hatchet? I don't want to be on edge whenever we talk."

Phil took a deep breath and calmed down. Bo extended a hand, and he took it in a firm handshake.

"Fine."

Doug smiled.

"What a warm sentiment."

The tension in the air died down, and Doug took over once more.

"Now that we're over that obstacle, what say we finish what we have to do here and leave? This isn't exactly the best place to have a conversation."

Steve nodded and left to get the loader. Bo opened up the trunk and lifted the bag filled with money. Phil stared at it with worry, and Doug walked up to him.

"Look, you know I trust you, right?"

Phil sighed and nodded.

"I know. It doesn't make me feel any less uneasy."

Doug clapped his old friend on the shoulder and smiled.

"Bo was the best choice. He has an office and runs a legitimate business. He also has a counter and a safe to keep the money in."

Doug watched Bo carry the bag out of the car and went on.

"Because of the nature of his business, no one will question him having large amounts of cash on hand. It's honestly the safest place the money could be. Don't worry about it."

Phil nodded along with Doug's explanation as Bo approached them. He noticed the look on Phil's face and walked up to him.

"You know, counting this could end up being a lot of work. I could use some help. What do you say?"

Phil looked up at Bo and smiled.

"I'd love to."

Doug nodded.

"Good decision. Just let Steve and me know when you guys are done counting, and we'll drop by. For now, let's get everything else done."

Bo turned to Phil.

"What are your tasks? I might as well help since you're helping me count the money."

"Follow me."

Phil and Bo stood over a burning metal barrel. The flames arched out and illuminated their faces.

"That is pretty hot."

Bo turned to Phil.

"What next?"

Phil produced the license plates from the getaway car and chucked them into the barrel.

"Now, we get rid of the evidence."

Doug walked up to them and dragged along a couple of trash bags.

"Is this all of it?"

Phil looked up and nodded.

"Steve and I searched every inch of the car and tossed everything we could find into those."

Doug handed the bags over to Phil, and together, he and Bo loaded them into the burning barrel. Sparks flew up to meet them, and the pair jumped backward.

"Whoa. That was a close shave."

Bo laughed despite how tense the situation was and settled on a smile. He stared at the fire and was mesmerized by the way it curled and arched with the wind.

"This is a pretty mellow way to end an otherwise hectic day."

Steve walked up to the group, and Doug looked up.

"What's the progress on the car?"

Steve gave a thumbs up.

"I loaded it into the compacter. I also went the extra mile removing the car doors. It'll get crushed a lot quicker."

Doug clapped his nephew on the shoulder.

"Good job."

Steve joined them by the fire and stared into the bright flames.

"All the trash went in?"

Phil nodded. The drum made a loud pop, and everyone took a step back.

"That would make your butt pucker."

Steve turned to Phil.

"Doug said you'll be counting the money with Bo now."

Bo nodded and gave a thumbs up.

"I could use the extra hands."

Steve smiled.

"So, how much do you think we got?"

Phil kept his eyes fixed on the flames as he responded.

"Enough to get out of this crappy town and start over somewhere. That's for sure."

Bo shrugged.

"We grabbed a lot of small bills, but the bag is hefty. It feels like a lot."

Steve smiled into the drum.

"I already know what I'm going to do with my cut of the loot."

He grabbed Phil's attention.

"What's that?"

Steve fantasized about all the things he could accomplish with a large amount of money. He could see all the scenarios playing out within the flames.

"The first thing I'm going to do is buy a new car. I'm tired of driving around beat-up vehicles that barely make it through a week."

Bo and Phil turned to each other with concerned expressions. Bo decided he would be the one to speak.

"Sorry to burst your bubble, but that's a terrible idea."

Steve looked up in surprise. The mental image of him driving a corvette shattered as he waited to hear more.

CHAPTER 12

THE TALLY

"Why is it a bad idea?"

Steve could not believe his idea had been shot down so quickly. Phil decided to explain.

"There's a lot of heat surrounding this money right now. If you buy something so expensive, so suddenly without a viable explanation for where you got the money. That will look more than a little suspicious."

Bo nodded.

"It just isn't the smartest thing to do. Besides, according to the plan, we aren't meant to touch any of the money for six months."

Steve ran his fingers through his dark brown hair, a look of disbelief clear on his face.

"Six months? Why the hell not?"

Bo stepped up and placed an arm on Steve's shoulder.

"Look, kid. I may be new to this game, and trust me, this will be my last stint. But even I know we need to let things settle before doing anything crazy."

Phil nodded in agreement.

"The cops are like a swarm of bees right now. It's best not to poke the hive."

The flames within the drum began to settle as the sun continued its journey to high noon. Steve kept his eyes fixed on the dying flames and found it eerily like his excitement, quickly dying. Bo turned to Phil.

"Is there anything else you need to do before we head out?"

Phil shook his head, and Bo turned to Steve.

"Alright, then. Phil and I are going to head out. You've got this, yeah?"

Steve looked up and nodded. Phil and Bo began to make their way up the beaten path.

"We'll reach out to you when we're done on this end. Till then, keep up appearances."

Bo waved over his shoulder, and Steve turned his attention back to the dying embers.

⊕

The Steamboat Police Department building hadn't been overhauled since it was built in the early seventies. Aside from an old addition and one small renovation after a storm, the building looked the same as when built. Still, it got the job done. Steamboat wasn't that large a city and didn't require a large police force. The police department was comprised of less than ten officers, all organized and led by the chief.

The main office area, known as 'the bullpen', housed several small desks pushed up against either side of the wall and separated by a single path down the middle. When the officers weren't out on patrol, they made use of the desks provided to them.

Andy sat at his desk on a hectic day, going through a ton of paperwork. He had been swamped since the parade. Unsurprising, given what happened that day. Andy glanced at his notepad for a brief second and went back to filing paper-work. He was so focused on what he was doing that he failed to notice the sheriff approaching his table.

Sheriff Mitchel was in his late fifties, but according to him, he was thirty-two at heart. The sheriff had an all-around jovial personality and got along great with the other officers in the department. Mitchel walked up to Andy's desk and whistled when he noticed his workload.

"I'd hate to be you right now."

Andy looked up and smiled.

"Sheriff Mitchel. I'm glad you could make it today."

Andy got up and took the sheriff's hand in a sturdy hand-shake.

"So, what's the status of the chief?"

Andy shrugged his shoulders.

"I've tried getting through to him. Still, no word."

Mitchel nodded and turned to the office at the head of the room.

"So, I'm guessing he isn't in right now?"

Andy shook his head.

"Why don't we head to his office and continue this conver-sation?"

Andy grabbed a few files from his desk and followed Mitchel as he walked into the chief's office. The desk was piled with paperwork, earning a soft whistle from Mitchel.

"The chief won't like this."

Andy sighed as he added the paperwork, he brought in with him to the pile.

"I hate to add to it."

Sheriff Mitchel took a vacant seat, and his expression turned serious.

"So, you're shorthanded this weekend?"

Andy nodded.

"Those two guys you sent my way were a huge help. Thanks again."

Mitchel shook his head and smiled.

"Happy to help. So, you say you haven't been able to get through to the chief?"

Andy nodded slowly.

"It's been hard to get through to him ever since he left for his vacation at the lake. I tried calling, but it went to voicemail."

Mitchel whistled.

"That'll be one hell of a voicemail to get."

Andy frowned.

"Which is why I didn't leave him one. I decided to call one of the officers. He's down at Steamboat Bank as we speak, gathering as much evidence as he can."

Mitchel nodded and stroked his chin as he did a little mental math.

"That brings your department down to six officers, if I'm not mistaken."

Andy sighed and leaned back in his seat.

"Yeah. It's been that way ever since the budget cuts. All the money went to the schools, and the police department took a large hit."

Andy shook his head.

"Now, only one officer per one thousand residents gets put on the payroll. We're extremely shorthanded."

Mitchel nodded understandingly.

"I know how you feel. I lost a few deputies a couple of years ago when the county was trying to get the auto plant to come here."

Mitchel laughed drily.

"They failed. Kentucky has cheaper land."

Andy chuckled and shook his head.

"Ain't that a bitch?"

He turned his attention to the paperwork laid out on the chief's desk and sobered.

"I've been on the force for a while now. I've seen my fair

share of strange cases, but this takes the cake."

Sheriff Mitchel adjusted in his seat and nodded.

"As soon as I got the report, I nearly fell out of my seat. Stuff like this doesn't usually happen around these parts."

The sheriff massaged the bridge of his nose and sighed.

"Have you called Major Case Crimes in St. Louis?"

Andy furrowed his eyebrows as he responded.

"It was a very tense call. They are willing to send down a rookie, fresh out of training. They want to know how much money is missing first before they consider escalating and sending down a whole squad."

Mitchel nodded understandingly.

"Small town crimes don't usually appeal to the big wigs. At least they are sending someone."

A bitter expression crossed the sheriff's face.

"All that matters is that we meet their quota."

Mitchel nodded.

"It's a harsh reality."

He glared at the papers before him and went on.

"This case, though, it rubs me the wrong may. These guys have to be the luckiest sons of bitches in existence."

Andy nodded.

"That, or they're pros. The robberies happened cleanly, and the time between each was very narrow."

Mitchel nodded in agreement.

"Shit, look at the route. All three banks are two-thirds of a mile from the other. They needed knowledge of Steamboat to be able to properly pull this off."

Andy gestured as he replied

"I was a lot more surprised when I was in the thick of things. I hadn't even gotten to the first bank when the second was called in. Pretty surprising stuff. Heck, after the third, I was half expecting a fourth robbery to be called in."

Mitchel sighed.

"We'll catch the culprits soon enough. Has the total been

taken yet? Do you know how much was stolen?"

Andy shook his head.

"Each bank needs to do a tally and get back to me. But they are so shaken up that I doubt I'll know till Monday."

Andy ran his fingers through his hair and sighed.

"Major Cases really needs that number. Hopefully, I can get it by Monday."

Mitchel slowly shook his head.

"What, so if it was just a couple of purses, they wouldn't bat an eyelash? Those suits don't get it. They don't want to play if it isn't a challenge."

Andy chuckled.

"I hear that."

He stared at the paperwork one last time and briskly rose from his seat.

"Well, whatever the case may be. I'm going to follow the clues and hunt down the bastards that did this. They certainly didn't make it easy, but someone is bound to slip up eventually."

Mitchel nodded slowly.

"Hope for a large crew. It's harder to keep tabs on everyone in a large crew. Eventually, one of them will crack and do something stupid. You can count on it."

Andy was a little puzzled.

"A large crew, huh? And what if that isn't the case? What if it's just three people? Or two?"

Mitchel snorted.

"Then pray for a miracle."

Andy stared up at the ceiling. The amount of pressure he felt was overwhelming. He turned to the sheriff.

"Have you ever felt helpless as the sheriff?"

Mitchel sighed as he turned to the window and gazed up at the clouds rolling over the police station.

"Only once. When that boy went missing for four years. The look on his parent's face when he returned though. Was like an anvil lifted off my shoulders. I don't know how this is going to feel."

#

Phil, Steve, and Bo were already gathered in Bo's trailer when Doug arrived. Phil stood silently in the corner and kept his eyes fixed on the table. Steve, on the other hand, failed to mask his excitement.

"Holy shit. That's a ton of cash."

Phil rolled his eyes.

"Calm down, boy. There isn't a big tittie blonde in here. It's just money."

Steve smirked.

"Those two aren't mutually exclusive. Where there's one, there's bound to be the other."

Doug walked in on the conversation and slowly shook his head.

"Boy, you've still got a lot to learn."

Bo looked up at Doug's arrival.

"Is the door locked?"

Phil reached out and turned the latch.

"It is now."

All attention was on the pile of money as silence fell over the room. The silence was palpable, and Steve couldn't take much more of it.

"Why is everyone so quiet?"

Steve eyed all of his associates as he asked the question. Bo adjusted in his seat and leaned back. Phil grabbed a chair himself and remained silent. Steve's eyes darted back and forth between Doug and Bo in demand of an answer.

"Well, Phil? Bo?"

Bo held his hands up.

"This may be my trailer, but I'm not the one in charge. Doug gets the final word."

Phil reached out and grabbed Steve by the shoulder.

"Exercise a little patience."

The money was arranged in four rows containing several stacks each. The stacks were reasonably tall, and all the money occupied the majority of Bo's desk. Doug eyed their loot and slowly stroked his chin.

"I guess it's now or never."

He turned to Bo.

"So, how much did we manage to make?"

Bo turned to Phil and smiled.

"Phil has the breakdown. I'm sure he would love to do the honors."

Phil clutched a sheet of paper firmly between his fingers and rose from his seat. He stepped over to the desk and took one last look at the cash before reading out the summary.

"Before I get into it, everyone did a great job. It was smooth sailing the entire time, and we all managed to pull this off."

He stared at the sheet of paper and went on.

"In total, we snagged four hundred and eighty-six thousand, seven hundred, and twelve dollars. When we divide that equally between four people, it comes to a hundred and twenty-one thousand, six hundred and seventy-eight dollars."

Steve's eyes widened, and his jaw dropped. Doug eyed the money and whistled.

"The total almost comes up to half a million dollars."

Phil slowly nodded his head.

"You can say that again."

Bo smiled and sighed.

"So, Doug. What's the plan? You're the brains behind this operation, and we've managed to get this far because of you. Your call on whatever the next steps you give."

Doug looked at the others and understood the same resolve in their eyes.

"You all feel the same way?"

They nodded, and he took a deep breath.

"Right. Now that we are all here let's go over the rules one more time."

Doug looked at each of his allies in the eyes as he went on.

"What happens in the next few months is crucial. So, we all must be clear on what to do. Now, listen up."

CHAPTER 13

SLIP UP

Doug cleared his throat and began.

"Just to be clear, in case we aren't all on the same page, no one touches this money for the next six months."

Bo and Phil nodded, each not phased. But it was clear that Steve wasn't entirely comfortable with Doug's order. Phil spoke up.

"That should be enough time for the heat to die down."

Doug nodded.

"In the meantime, it is important that nothing changes. We are trying to avoid suspicion, and even a slight change in our normal lives could draw attention."

Doug eyed his accomplices and went on.

"Before this, only Phil, Steve, and I had any known ties. Which means we won't be seeing Bo for some time. Steve did do some work for him but hold off on that just to be on the safe side."

All eyes turned to Bo, and he shrugged.

"No offense, but I look forward to it. Some time away from all this will do me a lot of good."

Doug grinned.

"Good. Now, it's important to know that no one suspects us yet. Let's keep it that way, alright?"

Everyone nodded in agreement, and Doug allowed himself an out of character smile.

"I can't believe we pulled this off without a hitch. Who would have thought a couple of beat-up cars and some road flares were all we needed?"

Doug laughed and shook his head. Bo and Phil shared in his joy.

"Heck, I thought we were done for at the last bank when that old man pulled up. But we managed to pull through."

Phil spoke up.

"I nearly shat myself when I heard sirens. I did not think we would make such a clean getaway."

The trio continued to discuss a call or two during the job while Steve wallowed in the corner. Doug settled and smirked.

"This was well done. For doing such a great job, I think it's only fair that we all get a small reward."

Steve's ears perked up at that. All eyes were on Doug at that moment, waiting to hear what he had in mind.

"We can't carry around this much money until the end of the six months, but it wouldn't hurt if we cut out a small percentage."

Doug picked up a collection of bills and weighed them in hand.

"Ten thousand each should be a good reward. Don't you think?"

Steve shot out of his seat with an excited smile on his face.
"Hell, yeah!"

Bo and Phil both nodded in agreement.

"That seems fair."

Steve sighed and fell back into his seat.

"My God, that was killing me. Six months is a long time."

Doug nodded understandingly.

"This doesn't mean we do anything stupid, mind you. Watch the way you spend it."

Doug tossed a hand full of bills to each of his accomplices. Bo thumbed through the money and made some mental calculations. Steve stared at the money, scared to grab on for fear of it disappearing. Phil fanned himself with his share and yawned.

Doug smirked and spoke up.

"Shit. I wish I had a beer right now. Seems like the best way to cap off a successful job."

Bo snapped his fingers and furrowed his eyebrows.

"And I just moved the fridge, too. I usually have drinks here for customers."

Phil shrugged.

"It's alright. Doesn't take away from the high."

Doug walked up to Steve and clapped him on the shoulder.

"Way to keep your shit together, boy. You really held a level head out there. I was afraid you'd do something stupid, but you stuck to the plan."

Steve smiled up at his uncle.

"That means a lot coming from you."

Phil and Bo shared a handshake, and the overall atmosphere remained upbeat for a long time.

Two weeks went by after the robberies with little progress being made. Andy worked around the clock, trying to gather some meaningful evidence. Unfortunately, it felt like the culprits had vanished into thin air.

In that time, the chief returned from his short vacation. Major Cases up in St. Louis sent down an officer to help with the investigation. On a particularly sunny Monday morning, Andy was at it again. He arrived at the station early and spent a good chunk of his time trying to make sense of the evidence and clues they had gathered from the three crime scenes.

A man in his early twenties, dressed in a gray suit and sporting a clean haircut, approached Andy's desk.

"Good morning, Andy. You're at it early again?"

Andy looked up and smiled.

"Morning, Jay."

Jay was fresh out of the academy in St. Louis. He was a little green, but he genuinely wanted to help.

"What are you doing here so early, rookie?"

Jay sighed and shook his head.

"We've been working together for almost two weeks now, and you still insist on calling me that."

Andy smiled and leaned back in his seat.

"For one, it ruffles your feathers, which I like. Secondly, you're still in your first year, so it's technically true."

Jay shook his head and shrugged.

"Whatever. Do you have a second?"

Andy nodded as he leaned forward.

"Sure, what's up?"

Jay eyed the room and frowned.

"Not here. Let's go talk in the chief's office."

Andy slowly shook his head.

"I don't want to disturb the chief with something unimportant."

Jay smiled.

"Trust me, it will be worth the trouble."

Andy eyed Jay for a few seconds and sighed.

"Fine. Let's go."

Jay led the way, his face fixed in a bright smile as they approached the chief's office. He knocked on the door and stuck his head in.

"Good morning, Chief. I might have something for you. Mind if we come in?"

Nathaniel Danvers, Chief of the Steamboat Police Department, was a heavy-set man in his early fifties. He favored white shirts and dark ties and held his pants up with suspenders. His hair was a deep brown, and he insisted on keeping a bushy mustache that hid much of his upper lip. The chief spoke up.

"Ah, Jay. Come on in."

The pair walked in on the chief in the middle of paperwork. He finished off on a document and set his pen aside as they walked in.

"Take a seat."

Jay and Andy reclined into their seats and waited for the chief to give the go ahead.

"So, what have you got for me?"

Jay sat forward excitedly.

"Alright. So, it's been two weeks since the robberies happened, and we haven't been able to turn up any solid leads yet."

Nathaniel leaned back in his seat and listened.

"The leads that we did manage to find were all dead ends. The two cars we found, one strangely parked across from Boatman's hasn't been registered in years and didn't have any DNA evidence in it. The same goes for the one left at Eagle's Nest. None of the bank workers could give solid descriptions of the perps, and the security cameras we checked were no help with all the perps wearing gloves and masks."

The chief grunted.

"Why are you telling me what I already know?"

Jay held his hand up and smiled.

"Sorry, I was building up to it. I discovered something that I want to run by you guys."

The chief nodded.

"Well, spit it out."

Jay took a deep breath.

"In a class back at the academy..."

Andy stifled a laugh and slowly shook his head.

"This ought to be good."

The chief shot Andy a glare, and he cleared his throat.

"Sorry about that. Go on."

Jay nodded.

"As I was saying. In my post-crime investigation class, the teacher laid out a couple of habits and tendencies of bank robbers after a job. Things like trying to flee the state with their prize, finding a safe place to stash the loot, and so on. One thing he said that really stuck with me is the urge to spend. It's almost irresistible."

Andy slowly shook his head.

"We covered that last week already, remember? You and I went through most of the transactions on record from the last week and didn't find anything out of the ordinary. I thought we already ruled this out as a possibility."

Jay shook his head.

"I couldn't shake the feeling that we missed something. So, I went through it again. When you and I canvased the records, we mostly paid attention to the large transactions. But then it hit me. What if the transaction wasn't large?"

Jay had managed to capture the chief's attention. Nathaniel leaned forward in his seat and spoke up.

"That sounds interesting. Unfortunately, we can't go through every single transaction in time, surely."

Jay turned to the chief and nodded.

"Yeah, that would be a huge waste of time. Fortunately, there are other ways of narrowing the list other than looking for a high price tag."

Jay retrieved a piece of paper from his file and laid it out on the table.

"The first thing I looked out for was major property purchases in the last two weeks. All the buyers checked out, so I moved on. The next big thing would be vehicles. I checked if there were any luxury cars paid for at that time. Nothing. Expensive trucks, muscle cars none of those were purchased in the last two weeks."

Andy leaned forward in his seat and smirked.

"So, what? Did you do farm machinery next?"

Jay thoughtfully stroked his chin.

"I actually didn't consider that. I'll add it to my list the next time I'm in a rural area."

The chief grew impatient.

"Mr. Jay, can you please get on with it? What did you find that my guys didn't?"

Jay nodded.

"Sorry, Chief. I decided to expand the radius of my search. I discovered a citation given not too long ago for a muscle car. It was possible someone bought the vehicle outside of town and shipped it in. The violation caught my attention, so I decided to look into the man involved."

The chief intertwined his fingers and focused on what Jay had to say.

"What was the ticket for?"

Jay retrieved the slip from his folder and read it out.

"No proof of registration for a vintage muscle car."

The chief leaned back in his seat.

"That doesn't sound suspicious."

Andy interjected.

"When was that issued?"

"Two days ago."

Andy scratched his head.

"On a Saturday?"

Jay nodded.

"Friday night, to be precise."

The chief asked another question.

"Who issued the citation?"

"The sheriff's deputy from the county over."

The chief seemed a tad skeptical.

"If it was issued in the next county, why is it suspicious?"

Jay leaned forward as he explained.

"It was enough to earn my attention, so I did some digging

on the man involved. His adult record is clean. His juvenile records were sealed, but I did notice a drug mark on the file. That isn't the interesting part."

The chief was once again interested.

"I hate to break off with a question, but could you tell me what you know about a local?"

Andy spoke up.

"Name?"

"Steve Harris."

Nathaniel stroked his chin as he considered the name.

"Doesn't ring a bell. Should I know who this is?"

Andy spoke up.

"I remember the name Harris from when I was a kid. It doesn't mean anything, though."

Jay smirked.

"His name may not ring a bell, but his father sure sticks out."

Andy and the chief shared a glance as Jay rifled through his folder once more. He spread it open and went on.

"Steve's dad was killed in Chicago years ago. It was around when the south side was like the wild west, teeming with criminal activity. His dad also had a record."

Andy slowly shook his head.

"I do not see a connection. So, Steve's dad had a criminal past. So, what? That doesn't mean this Steve Harris had anything to do with those robberies."

Jay returned the piece of paper to his folder and replied.

"I'm not that shallow minded. I just wanted to build up Steve's back story a little bit. What you should be concerned about is the fact that I couldn't find anything he has, so no stable means of employment that would allow him to afford that car."

CHAPTER 14

FOLLOWING THE CLUES

The chief paused and fell silent. He thought over the information Jay had offered before responding.

"While I see your point of view, I still don't think it's enough to look into him."

Jay paused and reached back into his folder.

"If that isn't enough to convince you, how about this?"

He produced a piece of paper and eyed it before reading.

"I traced down the seller and talked to him about the car and who he sold it to. He didn't have much to say, but he did state that Steve paid for the vehicle in cash."

Jay eyed the sheet closely and went on.

"One stack of hundred-dollar bills and the rest in small change. The seller found this a tad weird, which is why he remembered."

Jay looked up and could tell from the expression in the chief's eyes that he had grabbed his curiosity. Nathaniel stroked his chin and considered what to do next. Andy also looked interested and spoke up.

"How did you come across the seller?"

Jay shrugged.

"It was easy enough to do. The ticket report had the car details included. I just ran a search on Google and found the exact car still on Craigslist. From there, it was a simple matter of contacting the seller and arranging a phone call."

Andy looked impressed.

"How much did the kid pay for it?"

"The price on Craigslist was listed as twenty thousand, but the kid negotiated it down to seventeen. The seller was a little miffed about that when I questioned him."

Jay shook his head slowly.

"Seventeen thousand dollars is still a lot of money. Where does a kid without a steady job get that kind of money in cold, hard cash? "

Jay leaned back in his seat and frowned.

"Heck, I have a steady job, and I can't afford that. It just seems really fishy to me."

The chief nodded in agreement.

"It does sound fishy."

He turned to Andy.

"It looks like you and your best friend over here have a lead to follow. You know what to do."

The chief rose from his seat and reached out to take Jay's hand in a sturdy handshake.

"You did great, kid. If this lead pans out, we might be able to solve this case just yet."

Jay nodded and smiled.

"My pleasure, Chief."

Nathaniel settled back into his seat with a loud sigh.

"Off you go, then. Also, if you need anything at all, don't hesitate to let me know."

Jay nodded and rose from his seat as he turned to leave. Andy stared at the chief in disbelief and quickly comported himself before taking his leave.

Andy led Jay to his cruiser, and the latter sat in the

passenger's seat as Andy drove off. The pair rode in silence for the most part. Jay went over a few digital files on his phone and looked up after a while.

"Steve's last known address is his uncle's house. We should probably head there first."

A twinkle entered Jay's eyes, and he went on.

"So, I managed to dig up some info on the uncle. Guess what he does for a living?"

Andy shrugged and sighed.

"I don't know. Rob banks, maybe?"

Jay rolled his eyes.

"Very funny. You know, you could show a little more appreciation for this lead. All you've done so far is offer lame jokes."

Andy frowned and glared at the road ahead of them.

"Excuse me if I'm a bit skeptical. We've been working on this for weeks now and still haven't made any worthwhile progress."

Andy sighed and settled into his seat.

"All these people count on me to keep them safe; I can't afford to slip up again. You have no idea how helpless I felt during the robberies. I was there, but I was always one step behind them."

Andy gripped the wheel with both hands and made a sharp turn.

"I'm determined to fix this. The guilt, the shame, the way people look at me in public; it's a lot."

Jay noticed the sadness in Andy's eyes and calmed.

"You're being too hard on yourself. You did your best."

Andy slowly shook his head.

"My best wasn't good enough. Three banks were robbed on my watch."

Jay sighed.

"The people are being too hard on you. Surely, they realize that there was nothing you could have done."

Andy slowly shook his head.

"I don't blame them, honestly. You wouldn't understand. This is a small community."

Jay shrugged.

"So?"

Andy rolled his eyes.

"Exactly my point. You need to see this robbery from our standpoint. Steamboat is a small place with hardly any crime. Heck, natural disasters were the biggest travesties here until two weeks ago."

Jay settled into his seat and stared at the sky above them.

"You're right, I don't understand. I lived in Denver before I got enlisted at St. Louis. Denver is a pretty big place, and so is St. Louis. I don't know much about small towns."

Andy turned to Jay.

"Why would you leave Denver for St. Louis? That makes no sense."

Jay smiled to himself.

"Well, I really wanted to get into Major Case Crimes. Unfortunately, there were no openings in Denver. The St. Louis branch had an opening, so I thought, why not?"

Andy grunted.

"I know people that would kill to live in Denver. It's a big vacation destination for a lot of the folks around these parts, myself included."

Jay shook his head.

"Anyways, I'm as invested in solving this case as you are. Don't think it doesn't concern me just because I'm from Major Case Crimes."

Andy snorted.

"You haven't been at Major Case Crimes long enough. After a while, you'll lose touch with the little things. Hell, look at your superiors. They sent a rookie down here because they thought this town's problems weren't big picture enough."

Jay folded his arms as he responded.

"Well, I disagree with that. I'm still here, so that should show that I care, even just a little bit."

Andy shrugged.

"Sure."

Jay sighed and turned his attention back to the road.

"So, do you want to know something odd about where we're headed?"

Andy nodded.

"Shoot."

Jay rapped his fingers against the dashboard as he spoke.

"The place belongs to Doug. Doug has done two stints in prison. One at Potosi, the other at Jefferson City."

Andy whistled softly.

"Jeff City? That's a maximum-security penitentiary."

Jay nodded.

"Are you seeing a pattern, too?"

Andy frowned slightly.

"Do you really think these could be our guys?"

Jay leaned back in his seat as they drew closer to their destination.

"I don't know Steamboat well enough to come to that conclusion. This is your town; I'm just following clues."

Andy took the next turn and drew his car to a halt in front of an old bungalow. He gave the house a once over and smiled as he opened his door.

"Let's follow the clues, then."

Andy and Jay walked up to the house side by side, both shocked by its state. Andy carefully ascended the steps leading up to the porch and shouted a warning.

"Careful on those steps. It feels like they could give way at any time."

Jay was careful to place his weight on the edge of the steps as he climbed up. The pair came to a halt in front of the metal screen covering the entrance. The building was silent for the most part as Jay peered in through one of the front windows.

"I don't see anyone in there."

Andy sighed.

"Well, there's only one way to find out."

He rapped against the screen with his knuckles and spoke up.

"Hello, is there anyone in there?"

His question was met without a response, and he grew impatient.

"Hello? Is there anyone in there?"

Andy heard something stir behind the screen and an angry mumble emanated from the windows.

"I'm coming, sheesh. Keep your pants on."

Andy turned to Jay and gave him a thumbs up. Jay kept his ears open and heard cans being shifted as someone approached the metal screen. A latch was pulled aside, and the door swung open. Doug stared out of the door and squinted his eyes.

"Damn, that's bright."

He paused for a moment and allowed his eyes to adjust before properly assessing the situation. Doug noticed that one of his callers was an officer and kept a blank expression.

"How can I help you?"

Andy stepped up to respond.

"Sorry to bother you. Is Steve Harris here?"

Doug cussed in his head. He had no idea why the police were looking for Steve, but he knew it was bad news.

"No, he isn't here."

Jay nodded.

"We would like a word with him. Do you know when he will get back? We really need to talk to him."

Doug shrugged.

"What can I say? I haven't seen the kid all day. What do you want to talk to him about?"

Jay and Andy shared a look. Andy turned back to Doug.

"Oh, we just wanted to follow up with him about a

registration."

Doug furrowed his eyebrows, clearly confused. He slowly nodded his head as he replied.

"Alright. I'll let the boy know you stopped by."

Jay spoke up.

"Do you have any idea when he'll be back?"

Doug shrugged.

"As I said, I haven't seen the kid all day. I have no idea when he'll be back. He does what he wants."

Andy frowned and sighed.

"Alright, then. Thank you for your time. We'll get out of your hair."

Andy tapped Jay on the shoulder and gestured towards his police car. The pair carefully descended the steps and boarded the vehicle.

Doug watched as they drove away and didn't flinch until they had turned down the road.

"Fuck!"

He slammed his fist into the wooden door frame and winced once the pain registered. The rage in Doug's eyes was palpable, and his breathing was ragged. He took a deep breath to steady himself and walked back into the house, slamming the door behind him as he did so.

Later that day, the sound of a powerful engine echoed down the street. A car came into view at the top of the road, a blue muscle car with white stripes and shaded windows. The car crawled forward, making its way over to Doug's driveway.

Steve peeked his head out of the driver's window and gazed at the garage opening before him.

"Will it fit?"

He inched his car forward in a bid to keep it unscratched as he managed to get it into the garage. Once the car was carefully parked, Steve killed the engine, and sweet silence fell over the neighborhood.

The silence was quickly replaced by the sounds of the

evening as crickets came out to play. Steve triple-checked that both doors leading into the car were locked before pocketing the key and approaching the house. He whistled a soft, jovial tune under his breath.

Steve walked in through the front door and gently shut it behind him. For the most part, the room was dark, and it made it hard for him to see where he was going. Steve expertly maneuvered through the darkness and found the light switch. As soon as he flipped it on, Doug spoke.

"Where have you been?"

Steve jumped, surprised to see Doug seated not that far from him with a beer in hand. Doug looked scarily calm, and something about his disposition made Steve uncomfortable.

"Jesus! What are you doing sitting in the dark like that?"

Doug glared at Steve and shot out of his seat.

"I said, where have you been? What the hell did you do?"

Steve looked lost as he stared at his fuming uncle. He held his hands up in surrender also trying to block his strong beer breath.

"Calm down. What are you talking about? I just got here."

Doug paced back and forth, and Steve watched him while standing completely still, unaware of the storm that was headed his way.

CHAPTER 15

A LOUD MISTAKE

Doug continued to pace back and forth while muttering to himself under his breath. Steve wisely chose to stay silent. He had experience dealing with his uncle when he was angry and knew that talking only made things worse. Doug paused mid-stride and fixed Steve with a glare.

"Why were there two cops in here earlier? They were looking for you."

Steve remained silent for a brief moment. He didn't seem entirely surprised.

"I have no idea."

Doug nodded. A vein bulged angrily on his forehead as he responded.

"No idea, huh? Alright, then riddle me this. I just heard something loud and large come to a halt out there. Do you want to tell me what it is? Or you have no idea?"

Steve shuffled in place. It was clear that he was far from comfortable as he looked for the words.

"Well, I thought..."

Doug cut him off and held up his finger.

"What did we agree on in Bo's trailer? Refresh my memory."

Steve sighed.

"That we wouldn't spend the money."

Doug nodded.

"Right. So, in your head, I assume you heard 'spend the money'?"

Steve quickly shook his head.

"But I didn't..."

Doug held up his finger.

"I didn't say I was finished. If the cops are here, then it's because of your dumb ass. I commend you for not doing something stupid, and what do you go ahead and do? Something stupid! Why don't you ever listen to me?"

Doug ran his fingers through his hair and fumed as he resumed pacing. Steve could tell that he was in a lot of trouble and tried to salvage the situation.

"Look. Phil said not to buy anything new so we can keep under the radar, and I didn't!"

Doug looked up.

"So, Phil knows about this?"

Steve slowly shook his head.

"No, I was referring to when we were at the junkyard. We talked about what we would do with our shares, and he told me not to buy something new. Bo confirmed it. So, I thought..."

Doug chuckled drily and shook his head.

"No, Steve. Thinking is the furthest thing from what you did. Did you even pay attention to the rest of what they had to say? Or did you just pick and choose what would benefit you?"

Doug took a step forward.

"Thanks to your recklessness, two lawmen showed up at my house this afternoon!"

Steve held up his hand and tried to explain.

"I didn't even get it around here. I went over to Illinois so it wouldn't draw attention."

Doug elevated his pitch slightly.

"Where did you get it from?"

Steve sighed and kicked against the carpet.

"A guy on Craigslist. I decided on that to avoid leaving a paper trail."

Doug palmed his face and slowly shook his head.

"You clearly didn't think this through. Any car within your possession requires papers, Steve! Whether or not you bought it on Craigslist or another state. You idiot!"

Doug took a deep breath and folded his arms.

"So, how did those two police officers know to come here? How did they know about your little car?"

Steve hung his head and stared at the carpet as he responded.

"I- I got pulled over on my way back for not having any plates."

Steve noticed Doug's face turning red and braced for impact. Doug kicked over the coffee table and tossed a nearby lamp to the floor. He picked up two cushions from the couch and tossed it at Steve. Steve deflected the pillows and remained standing, waiting for Doug to speak.

"How stupid can one person be? Damn it!"

Doug's breathing was erratic. His chest rose and fell as he glared at Steve without saying a word. He calmed slightly, spit foaming at the corners of his mouth as he continued to gasp for air.

"The car is here?"

Steve nodded slowly.

"Get it into the garage and shut the doors before someone sees."

Steve turned on his heels without a word and dashed out the front door. He grabbed the garage door handle and yanked it down, checking every second for an on-looker.

Satisfied that no one was watching, Steve returned to the house and walked in on Doug, pacing back and forth. He looked up as Steve walked in and sighed before taking a seat.

"Shut the door and take a seat."

Doug grabbed a bottle of beer sitting on the righted coffee table and took a long swig. Steve eyed another bottle on the coffee table and instinctively reached for it.

"Already drank it. Don't bother."

Steve drew his hand back and nodded. Doug took a deep breath and steadied himself.

"I need you to realize that what you did has put us in danger."

Steve slowly shook his head.

"Don't you think you're being a tad dramatic? So, I got a ticket, so what?"

Doug shook his head and chuckled.

"If only it were that simple."

He leaned forward and continued to speak.

"Your actions have set off a chain reaction that could doom us all."

Steve remained skeptical and oblivious.

"What would that be?"

Doug leaned back in his seat and took another drink from his beer.

"There's no way of telling, but one thing is certain. You can't keep the car. It needs to go."

A look of deep hurt and disappointment crossed Steve's face.

"What? No, it doesn't! Why do I need to get rid of it?"

Doug reached over and flicked Steve on the forehead.

"Hey! What was that for?"

"Think for a second. Say you keep the car. How do you explain having enough money to afford it? The car ties you to the money you used to pay for it; money you have no way of verifying as hard-earned."

Steve fell silent. It hadn't dawned on him he would need an explanation for the money. He rested his face in his open palms, and Doug laughed.

"You don't have an answer, do you? That's what I thought."

Steve looked up suddenly.

"I could make something up. It's not that hard."

Doug slowly shook his head.

"This isn't some friend you owe money. We're talking about the police here."

Steve thought through various excuses and snapped his fingers.

"I could say I won it at the casino over in Illinois. That's where I've been since Friday, anyways."

Doug set down his beer and smacked his forehead.

"You really think that will work?"

Steve seemed confident as he nodded his head.

"Did you win any money?"

Steve's smile deflated slightly.

"Well, not big really. But..."

Doug cut him short.

"But nothing. What, you don't think the casino keeps records of stuff like that? Plus, that place has cameras watching every angle. The police won't even need to take the casino at their word. They can just watch you not really winning at the games in glorious HD."

Steve fell silent once more as he considered his other options. Doug rested his chin against his knuckles and spoke up.

"How much did you pay for the car, anyway?"

Steve ignored the question as he spoke up.

"I tried to be as careful as possible. I thought I had all my bases covered."

Doug chuckled and shook his head.

"Well, clearly, you didn't. That's why we made a plan not to spend any of the cash for six months. If I had only been dealing with Phil and Bo, I probably wouldn't have had to come up with that rule. The one person it applied to the most ignored it entirely."

Steve crossed his arms and set his chin in a fit of stubbornness. Doug continued to glare daggers at him.

"You need to get rid of that car tonight. The sooner, the better. I can't have something that hot sitting in my garage. Understand?"

Steve looked up in surprise.

"Tonight?"

Doug nodded curtly.

"Yes. It's dark out, so it should be easier for you to get it out without anyone noticing. Judging by the sound, that won't matter much, but it should still give you a small advantage."

Steve slowly shook his head.

"I'll need help if you want me to get it out of here tonight."

Doug shrugged and leaned back in his seat.

"Then go find help. Just don't expect any from me."

Steve stared at his uncle in disbelief as he drank from his beer.

"But, we're family. Aren't we meant to help each other out of sticky situations like this?"

Doug set down the bottle once more.

"Family shouldn't be an excuse to be stupid. Now, you chose to be stupid, and I'm choosing to let you face the consequences on your own. That way, you'll learn. Who says I'm not a great uncle?"

Steve shot out of his seat and fumed as he stormed off towards the door. He paused with his hands on the handle and turned.

"So, you really aren't going to lift a finger?"

Doug smiled, showing little teeth in the process.

"The only thing I'm going to lift is this beer to my mouth."

Steve tossed his hands in the air, exasperatedly.

"This is bullshit. I can't believe you and I are related."

He glared at the door, fighting back the tears as he did so.

"So, this is on me alone? No problem. I'll show you I can fix my own messes."

Steve yanked open the door and Doug looked up.

"You never answered me. How much was the fucking car?"

Steve turned and walked out with his back first.

"It was seventeen thousand dollars."

Steve slammed the door behind him, and silence fell over the room in his absence. Doug sighed as he set down his beer. He gently held onto his head as he tried to ease his anxiety.

"We're fucked."

⊕

Doug pulled up to the parking lot in a beat-up truck. He shut off the engine and checked his watch to make sure he was on time. Doug had a good view of the building across the street. It was a place he was familiar with, but one he did not look forward to seeing.

"Desperate times."

Doug was confident that the AA meeting was close to completion. He sat in the truck for a few minutes and got out when he noticed the first person exit the building. The lady walked down the sidewalk and headed to the nearest row of cars.

Two men walked out after her and fired up smokes right next to the entrance. Doug approached and stood under a tree. He kept a close watch on the entrance and didn't shift until Phil stepped out.

Phil was talking with one of the members but paused when he noticed Doug standing in the shade.

"Let's continue this conversation next week."

Phil cautiously walked over to Doug with a smile on his face.

"You haven't shown up here in a long time. Finally, ready

to quit drinking?"

Doug shook his head.

"We might have a problem."

Phil's smile deflated, and he walked within whispering distance of Doug. The pair ensured they weren't being listened to before conversing. Phil asked the critical question.

"What's the problem?"

Doug glared off into the distance.

"It turns out my nephew has a lot more in common with his father than I originally thought. Idiots."

Phil held his hand up.

"Calm down and tell me what happened."

Doug took a deep breath and sighed.

"The damn kid brought some heat my way yesterday. He bought some kind of muscle car and got pulled over for not having plates."

Phil's eyes widened, and he ran his fingers through his hair. Doug went on.

"I found out about it after getting a delightful visit from two lawmen. It wasn't pleasant."

Phil was on the verge of exploding.

"What the fu..."

Doug cut him short.

"That isn't even the best part. Guess how much he paid for the damn thing?"

Phil didn't think he wanted to know, but he asked.

"How much?"

"Seventeen big ones."

CHAPTER 16

CLOSER TO THE TRUTH

Phil paced back and forth as he digested the information Doug gave him.

"Seventeen thousand? On a car?"

Doug nodded.

"I know, right? Anyways, I told him he had to get rid of the thing."

Phil took a deep breath and nodded.

"That's the smart move. Best not to draw any more attention to your place."

Doug sighed.

"He wasn't happy about it; stormed out of the place last night. I haven't seen him since."

Phil stroked his chin as he responded.

"Where the hell did he get seventeen thousand dollars? We agreed on ten, didn't we?"

Doug nodded.

"I was wondering the same thing. Steve said he was at the casino all weekend, but he didn't win anything real big. If anything, he should have less than ten on him. So, where did he get the extra cash? I was hoping you would have an idea."

Phil's eyes doubled in size, and he began to pace.

"Oh, man. I told him not to."

Doug looked up.

"Not to buy a car? He told me that much."

Phil shook his head.

"Not that. I told him not to take any money."

Doug placed his hand in Phil's path and fixed him with a severe gaze.

"Stop. What are you talking about?"

Phil leaned against the tree they were standing under and stared at the sky as he went on.

"Not to take any money. It was at Boatman's Bank. I saw the kid staring at a bunch of hundreds like it was a bag of candy. I told him not to take it because there might have been a dye pack in it. Or a tracer."

Doug nodded along.

"I figured he listened, so I turned and left. He was right behind me when the old man pulled up to the drive-through, so I didn't think much about it after."

Doug glared off into the distance.

"Son of a bitch!"

Doug began to pace and repeatedly ran his fingers through his hair as he considered their next move. Phil spoke up.

"Have you said anything to Bo about this?"

Doug sighed and slowly shook his head.

"We all agreed not to see each other. There's no sense in breaking that rule if it isn't absolutely important."

Phil nodded.

"Looks like we're on our own unless this escalates."

Doug kicked a nearby trashcan and watched it clatter to the ground.

"I went over this several times! Does the kid have lead in his ears?"

Phil held his hands up.

"Keep your voice down. Someone might hear you."

Doug looked about and calmed down.

"This plan wasn't exactly rocket science. It was simple and straightforward. Why doesn't he listen?"

Phil folded his arms and focused on Doug.

"So, what do you want to do?"

Doug sighed for the umpteenth time since his conversation with Phil began. He fell silent as he considered what to do next.

"I don't know yet. I'll wait for the kid to get back and see if he manages to handle the car problem without messing up. We move from there."

Phil nodded.

"Alright, then. Keep me informed."

Doug turned to leave and nodded.

"Will do."

⯁

Steve pulled his car up to Bo's trailer. He parked in the driveway and ran up the front steps, barging into the door.

"Bo, you've got to help me!"

Bo looked up from his desk in surprise. He was working on a blueprint and didn't expect anyone to visit.

"What are you doing here, kid? We aren't meant to see each other for six months! Did that somehow slip your mind?"

Steve shut the door behind him and walked up to Bo's desk.

"I know, I know. But I didn't know where else to go. I really need your help."

Bo sighed and massaged the bridge of his nose. He figured the best thing to do was listen to Steve and get him out of his trailer as quickly as possible.

"Fine. What do you need help with?"

Steve paced in front of Bo's desk and muttered to himself

as he did so.

"I've thought about it extensively, and this seems to be the best option."

He looked up and went on.

"I need you to say I work for you."

Bo was genuinely confused. He had no idea what Steve was going on about and needed clarification.

"Wait, what? Why?"

Steve came to a halt and took a deep breath.

"Let me just start from the beginning. See, I bought a car, the one outside..."

Bo's eyes doubled in size, and his mouth nearly hit the floor.

"You did what?"

Bo rushed out from behind his desk and over to a nearby window. He peeked through the blinds and eyed the blue car with white stripes parked out front. Bo felt a headache coming along. He could see the plan unraveling and did not like the feeling deep in the pit of his stomach.

Bo began to pace in front of the window, chastising himself for his predicament.

"What the hell was I thinking? Getting involved in all of this. It's over. It's all over."

Steve didn't see what the problem was and even smiled.

"No, it can be fixed. See, the way Doug explained it, I just need a verified income source to account for the money I spent on the car. That's where you come in. So, if anyone comes here, just say I'm working for you. Problem solved."

Bo turned to Steve and gave him an exasperated stare.

"You don't get it, Steve. I took out a larger than normal loan for the last few building projects my firm embarked on. If not for the patient contractors under me, the company would have gone under by now. Why do you think I was inclined to join you guys? Why would I risk everything I've worked so hard for if I had this shit all together?"

Steve stared at Bo blankly. It was clear that he still didn't understand what was happening.

"Let me be frank. I can't say you work here. Do you want to know why?"

Steve furrowed his eyebrows and nodded.

"The first and biggest reason is I cannot afford to pay you the amount of money needed for you to be able to afford that car out front."

Steve was about to speak up, but Bo held up his finger.

"Let me finish. Secondly, I have contractors that work on different sites every day. If the cops do some further investigating, the guys will say they have never seen you on site. It just has too many holes to be a viable option. Do you understand?"

Steve spoke up.

"But…"

Bo firmly shook his head.

"No buts. I'm not getting into trouble because you did something stupid. There's no sense in us both going down. You're just going to have to think up a solution on your own."

Bo's words cut Steve deeply, and he winced. It was clear that he was hurt and still oblivious to Bo's situation.

"Why did I even come here? I figured you would help me because you've been nice to me in the past. But no. You sound just like my asshole of an uncle."

Steve turned and trudged off to the door. He firmly gripped the handle and turned on Bo with rage-filled eyes.

"You both can burn in hell for all I care."

With that said, he yanked it open and stormed out.

⌖

Jay was on his way to the small Airbnb room he had been renting since coming to Steamboat. After another day of working on the case, he was ready to kick back and relax. He turned onto Klondike Road and continued down, whistling along with the song playing on the radio.

Jay turned to the left and noticed something familiar flash in his periphery. Jay slammed his foot down on the brakes, and his car screeched to a halt. He turned back and noticed the back end of Bo's trailer.

"I saw something."

The road seemed free. So, Jay put his car in reverse and slowly made his way back to Bo's trailer. The parking lot in front of the trailer came into view, and Jay noticed a blue muscle car parked out front.

Jay's eyes doubled in size as he pointed at the car.

"Andy isn't going to believe this."

Jay reached for his phone and dialed a number. He kept his eyes fixed on the car as the phone rang and smiled when the call went through.

"I found it."

Andy's voice came through the receiver.

"Where are you?"

"Klondike Road. Hurry."

Jay dropped the phone and realized he couldn't wait in the middle of the road. He turned around and went back to the nearby large white building, parking in their lot. While he waited for Andy, Jay tried to make sense of what he had seen. He wondered what the car was doing parked in the middle of nowhere.

Andy met Jay at the Knights of Columbus Hall in the parking lot.

"Get in."

Jay hopped out of his car and settled in beside Andy.

"Are you sure? Did you get a close look at it?"

Jay nodded as Andy drove out of the lot.

"No doubt about it. It's the same car from the ad. I recognized it from all the pictures."

Andy eyed the road ahead and furrowed his eyebrows.

"Where was it again?"

Jay leaned forward in his seat and squinted.

"It was parked in front of a mobile home, or something. You guys have tiny houses down here. Anyways, it shouldn't be hard to spot."

Andy smiled and shook his head.

"Most folks down here can't afford the big houses you're used to, nor do they want them. Most of us prefer the simple life."

Jay nodded slowly.

"Yeah, I forget that sometimes. Anyway, this thing looked like it was freshly built. The concrete looked good as new."

Jay kept his eyes fixed on the road ahead as he spoke. Soon, Bo's trailer came into view, and Jay's eyes widened. He pointed at the trailer and tapped Andy on the shoulder.

"There it is."

The parking lot came into view shortly after, but the muscle car was long gone. Jay frowned.

"But the car isn't there."

Andy stared at the trailer skeptically.

"Are you sure it was parked in front of that trailer specifically?"

Jay nodded and turned.

"I'm positive. Why?"

Andy stared at the trailer carefully and shook his head.

"That isn't home. That's the office of a private contractor."

Jay's eyes doubled in size.

"So, you know who's it is?"

Andy calmly nodded.

"I know who owns the trailer, but he doesn't own a car fitting that description. Not as far as I know."

Jay eyed the trailer closely and shrugged.

"Well, the car couldn't have gotten very far. Is this the only road out of town?"

Andy adjusted in his seat and nodded.

"Yes. It goes right past the Tiff mines, then you hit the county line, and it's nothing but open country after that."

Jay smiled excitedly.

"Well, let's go find us a vintage muscle car."

Andy put on the police siren and slammed his foot down on the gas. The car tires screeched, and the vehicle shot forward at a terrific speed. Buildings blurred by Andy's periphery, and he kept the car straight as they continued down the road.

Andy noticed the railroad track and knew the Tiff mines were in the distance and furrowed his eyebrows.

"Hopefully, we can catch him before he gets out of the county."

The cruiser maintained its speed, and soon, the tail lights of the vintage muscle car came into view.

"That should be the car."

Andy nodded.

"Hold on to your horses."

The distance between the cop car and Steve's car lessened with time, and soon, Andy had the vehicle right behind the muscle car. The brake light came on, and both vehicles came to a halt on the side of the road.

CHAPTER 17

IN PURSUIT

Andy and Jay kept watch of the car parked in front of them. Jay was on edge.

"This is exciting. How do we proceed?"

Andy eyed the vehicle carefully and slowly nodded to himself.

"Sit tight and observe. The driver seems to be alone, so I should be able to handle this."

Jay seemed uncertain.

"Are you sure? It wouldn't hurt to have some backup."

Andy nodded.

"I'm sure. Plus, we have no idea who's in the car."

Jay nodded.

"That's true. So, what's your plan of approach."

Andy unlocked the doors of the cruiser and set one foot out.

"It's best to make this look like a normal traffic stop and see where it goes from there."

Jay scratched the top of his head.

"Will that work?"

Andy nodded as he stepped out of the car.

"Of course."

Andy stepped out of the vehicle, and Jay watched as he cautiously approached the muscle car.

⊕

Steve ran his fingers through his hair as he barreled down the street. He thought back to his conversation with Bo and boiled with anger.

"Was the idea of helping me so crazy?"

Steve couldn't think clearly. He felt nothing but anger towards Bo and his uncle.

"I'll show them. There must be a way out of this."

Steve paid no attention to his driving and ended up going pretty fast. He was so oblivious to his surroundings. He didn't register the sound of police sirens until the flashing red and blue lights enveloped his car in a shifting overlay of colors.

Steve looked up when the sound became more pronounced and quickly snapped back to the present.

"What the?"

He briefly glanced in his rearview mirror and noticed a police car hot on his tail.

"Crap. I don't need this right now. What do I do?"

Steve briefly considered gunning his engines and making a run for it, but quickly thought against it.

"That'll just make me look guilty."

He took a deep breath and calmed his mind.

"I can do this. I just need to relax and play it cool."

Steve gently eased his pressure on the gas pedal, and his car slowed. He came to a stop by the roadside, and the cop car on his tail stopped right behind him. Steve sat up in his seat and eyed the side window. He peered at the police car and noticed some movement in the driver's seat.

"Ok, just play it cool. Remember, you have nothing to

hide."

Steve kept his hands on the steering wheel as a police officer approached the driver's side of the car.

⊕

Andy walked up to the muscle car and took note of a few details. He noticed the windows were slightly tinted.

"The color fits the description Jay dug up. Now, to see who is behind the wheel."

Andy walked up to the driver's window with his thumbs tucked into his belt. He kept a blank expression and gazed down at the driver. Steve looked up from his seat and fixed on his brightest smile.

"Good day, officer. A pleasant afternoon for a drive, don't you think?"

Andy noted the age and facial features of the driver and committed that information to memory. He maintained his blank expression as he replied.

"Good afternoon, sir. Are you aware that you were doing fifty in a thirty-mph zone?"

Steve chided himself for neglecting the speed limit. Sitting with an officer just a few feet away made him extremely uncomfortable, but he decided to bear with it so he could get away as fast as possible.

"Sorry about that, sir. I'm still not used to the power of this engine."

Andy lifted a single eyebrow and eyed the hood of the car.

"That's a nice ride you've got there. Is it new?"

Steve nodded slowly.

"Sort of new but also old, 392 underneath."

Andy straightened himself and returned his pen and notepad to his pouch.

"Can I see your license and registration, please?"

Steve groaned and leaned forward in his seat. He produced

his wallet and brought out his driver's license.

"Here's my license, sir."

Andy grabbed the card and held it up to the light. His eyes paused over the name, and he managed to hide his excitement.

Jackpot.

Andy handed the card back and nodded as he continued.

"And your registration?"

Steve ran his fingers through his hair and sighed.

"Sorry. But I don't have that yet. I just got this car a few days ago. I haven't gotten around to getting the right papers yet."

Andy smiled to himself. As he had guessed, Steve didn't have the necessary papers.

"Sir, I'm going to have to ask you to step out of the vehicle."

Steve looked up in surprise.

"What, why? I was just a little over the speed limit."

Andy stepped back and gestured with his hand and arm.

"Please, step out."

Steve groaned and palmed his face.

"Fine."

He departed out of the car, and Andy pointed to the roof.

"You were doing more than a little over the speed limit. We are looking for someone matching your description of driving a vintage muscle car. Please place your hands on the roof and spread your legs."

Steve did as he was told, but his mind raced for a solution. He could not believe he was on the verge of being arrested.

He thought. "I can't go to jail. Why did it have to end like this?"

Steve eyed his surroundings, thinking of a way to get out of his predicament. Andy turned to his car and gave Jay a thumbs up. Jay could tell from the scene before him they had gotten their guy.

Jay says to himself. "We just need to get him back to the

station. Shouldn't be a problem, since his license plate is missing."

Andy stepped to the back of the car and eyed the missing slot. He slowly shook his head and spoke up.

"I won't lie. This isn't looking good. No papers and your plates are missing. I'm afraid I'm going to need to take you back to the station for further questioning."

Steve's head was spinning as he thought of the possible outcomes of that trip. He did not want to be in a police station, not after what he and his accomplices had done. Steve turned away from the police car and noticed a break in the fence on the side of the road. He once again considered making a break for it.

This time, Steve summoned courage and ran. Andy looked up, surprised by the sudden burst of movement.

Andy yells. "Hey, where do you think you're going?"

Jay undid his seat belt and exited the car.

Jay shouts. "He's getting away. After him."

Steve launched himself through the fence and ran through the woods on the other side.

"We could lose him in there. Pick up the pace."

Andy and Jay were right on his tail and followed him through the woods. Andy was determined not to lose his target and ran as fast as his legs could take him.

Steve noticed a break in the trees a few feet away and jumped through. He landed running through a field on a farm, and made his way over to the tractor at the center. Andy and Jay got out of the woods a few feet behind him and scanned the area. Jay pointed towards the center of the farm.

"There he goes."

Andy held his hand out and yelled at the top of his lungs.

"Hey! Stop! Come back here!"

Steve ignored the call and mantled over the tractor at the center of the farm.

"Damn it, he isn't stopping."

Jay gasped as he kept up with Andy.

"We need to catch up to him. Pick up the pace."

Andy kicked things up a gear and shot forward. Jay struggled to keep up and stayed close behind him. Andy was almost to the tractor, trying to gain on Steve in the open area, and Jay did what he could with a major effort. Once they were past the machine, Andy came to a sudden stop. Jay bumped into Andy and keeled over.

"What's the hold up?"

Andy glared and stared off into the distance.

"I lost sight of the kid."

Jay stood up and helped search for their target. He spotted a figure drop down in the distance and pointed.

"That way."

The pair ran for the location, and Andy's eyes widened. He came to a sudden halt again and held Jay back. Jay eyed the dry creek embankment in front of them and gasped.

"If we rush down that thing, we could land badly."

Andy spotted Steve coming up on the other side of the embankment and glared.

"Come on! Watch your step."

The embankment was steep with loose soil and roots popping out, and after slowly sliding to the bottom, the pair could get their bearings. Andy and Jay climbed up the other side as quickly as possible and managed to make it out.

"Where'd he go this time?"

Andy eyed the hill before them and spotted Steve halfway up. He pointed at it and continued forward, closely followed by a wheezing Jay. Andy was extra careful as they climbed the hill and kept his eyes fixed on Steve. The pair came to a leveled foothold and paused. Steve looked down at the men chasing him and frowned.

"Why won't they get lost?"

He was on the verge of diving into a nearby bush and decided on a different course of action. Steve grabbed his hoodie and reached into it. Andy noticed and held his hand up.

"Whoa, Kid. Don't do it. It doesn't have to come down to that."

Steve's hand traveled deeper into his hoodie, and he turned to face Andy and Jay as he yanked. The pair brandished their standard-issue pistols, and both took shots at Steve. The sound traveled through the quiet day and eventually fell off in the distance.

Steve's eyes doubled in size for a moment before he fell to the ground. Jay paused and keeled over, taking a moment to catch his breath. Andy seemed to be just fine and carefully approached Steve's body.

Andy holstered his weapon, but Jay kept his handy as they walked up to the body. Andy carefully eyed Steve at his feet, and his eyes softened.

"You can put that away now. I doubt the kid can harm you with that."

Jay turned to Andy in confusion.

"Wait, what?"

Andy rolled Steve over and pointed at the weapon in his hand.

"He wasn't pulling out a gun. It was a socket wrench."

Andy ran his fingers through his hair and sighed as he stepped to the side. He sat on a large rock and gazed off into the overcast sky. Jay cautiously approached the body and stared down at it. He noticed the socket wrench and felt guilt wash over him.

Jay finally put his gun away and turned to Andy.

"I thought..."

Andy nodded.

"I know. I thought the same thing. We were both wrong."

Jay seemed a bit concerned.

"So, what does this mean? What do we do next?"

Andy carefully considered the question.

"First, we need to report the shooting."

He got up from his seat and crouched in front of Steve's body.

"If he isn't the guy we were after, then we have a lot of explaining to do."

Jay frowned, and Andy pulled out his cell phone, one-touch dialed.

"Dispatch, can you hear me?"

Jay walked over to the large rock and plopped down. He was clearly distraught by what happened and fought to keep his emotions in check as Andy made the call.

"We engaged a possible suspect, and shots were fired. The suspect is down. I'm requesting medical assistance."

Andy paused and listened to the response.

"We aren't that far from the Tiff mines."

Andy listened again for a short moment before responding.

"Awesome. Also, please put me through to the chief."

Andy turned to the body and frowned.

"He's not going to like this."

CHAPTER 18

REPORTING A SHOOTING

Chief Danvers stood, gazing at the clear sky outside of his window. He had a lot on his mind with the currently hanging case and needed a clear mind. The chief's concentration was disrupted by his ringing phone, and he glared at the receiver.

"Amanda, I told you to hold all my calls."

The chief's assistant scurried into the room, looking flustered.

"It's Andy, sir. It sounded very important, so I put him through."

Nathaniel sighed and nodded.

"Alright."

He took a deep breath and picked up the receiver.

"Chief, are you there?"

Chief Danvers reclined in his seat with a large sigh.

"Yeah, Andy. What have you got for me?"

"We found Steve and the muscle car."

Nathaniel leaned forward in his seat and smiled.

"That's great news. Bring him in."

Andy sighed over the phone.

"That won't be possible, I'm afraid. He didn't make it."

Nathaniel stopped himself from swearing as he glared off into the distance.

"What the hell happened? Start from the beginning."

"Well, Jay found the car parked in front of a job trailer. When I finally got here, the car was gone. So, we drove off in search of it. We finally caught up to him near the old Tiff mines. I pulled Steve over, but he panicked and ran."

Nathaniel nodded along.

"So, you gave chase?"

"Yeah. Jay and I ran after the kid. We chased him through the woods to a hill behind this old farm, across an old dry creek bed. I noticed him reach for something in his hoodie and immediately drew my weapon. Jay did the same, and we dropped him."

Chief Danvers was surprised by the conclusion.

"You didn't aim for his shoulder? You should know that by now."

Andy responded.

"I did. Chief. But Jay didn't. He hit the kid right in the chest."

Andy paused for a moment and went on.

"He had a socket wrench under his hoodie. It wasn't a gun."

Nathaniel Danvers nodded.

"Don't beat yourself up about it."

Andy sighed over the line and went on.

"I didn't think to tell Jay about our practices. Now, we're down one suspect."

Chief Danvers leaned back in his seat and stared at the ceiling.

"He's still new. He'll learn from this. Don't sweat the small stuff. We'll debrief when the two of you get back. Where are you now?"

"We waited for the EMT's to arrive. Now, we're on our way

back to Steve's uncle's place. If anyone is going to tell him his nephew died, we should."

Nathaniel Danvers hated how complicated things were getting. He massaged the bridge of his nose and shut his eyes as Andy went on.

"The thing is, Jay said he saw the car parked in front of Bo's job trailer."

Chief Danvers lifted a single eyebrow as he responded.

"Oh? I wonder what he was doing there."

"I was wondering the same thing. Jay and I will drop by and see Bo once we're done with Doug."

Nathaniel fell silent for a moment as he thought of the situation.

"You know what? Don't worry about Bo. I'll go visit him myself."

"Are you sure?"

Nathaniel nodded to no one in particular.

"A visit is long overdue. I just hope he hasn't gotten mixed up in all of this nonsense. We still don't know if Steve was one of the robbers."

"Alright. Understood."

Andy hung up, and the chief returned the phone to its rocker. He stared at it, deep in thought, and considered his next move.

"There's no sense in putting it off."

Nathaniel got up from his seat and grabbed his coat off the rack.

"Time to see what Bo is up to."

⊕

Bo smiled as he spoke on the phone. He was on the verge of closing another contract, and things were looking great. Bo had been a little worried after his run-in with Steve earlier, but he was in a much better mood.

"It's almost done. All that's left is the finishing touches."

Bo fell silent and chuckled.

"I know. I'm as excited as you are."

A knock came on Bo's door amid the conversation, and he looked up.

"Come in. The door is open."

Bo watched, wide-eyed, as Chief Danvers walked into his trailer. Bo was immediately worried but managed to keep a straight face as he listened to his caller.

"You know what? How about we talk about it when we close in a few days?"

Bo paused and nodded.

"Yeah. Someone very important just walked into my trailer. I'll talk to you later."

Bo put down his cell phone and looked up at his guest. He noticed the chief going over a few plans on the table in the next room and took a moment to calm down. Bo took a deep breath and got up with a passive expression. He walked into the next room and smiled as he held out his hands.

"Chief Danvers. What a pleasant surprise."

The chief took Bo's hand in a firm handshake but did not smile.

"Pretty good, considering all the chaos."

Bo immediately lost his smile and nodded.

"Yeah. It's been a crazy couple of weeks."

Bo gestured to a seat and sat opposite his guest.

"So, to what do I owe the pleasure of your visit?"

Nathaniel Danvers leaned back in his seat and passively stared at Bo.

"Well, I'm not here to talk about houses."

Bo nodded sheepishly as he licked his lips.

"Look. Something was brought to my attention that I need to look into. Now, I know you make some of the best houses this town has ever seen. But that doesn't make you exempt from the law."

Bo shifted in his seat and casually crossed his legs.

"Of course not. Did something happen?"

Chief Danvers nodded.

"Did you hear about the robberies that happened a few weeks ago?"

Bo hid his shock at the question and kept a straight face as he answered.

"It was all over the papers for weeks. Hard to miss. Heck, I couldn't even go down to the diner for a decent cup of coffee without the old-timers discussing it."

Chief Danvers smiled.

"Well, they do love to talk at that café."

Bo chuckled and shook his head.

"Yup, they do."

Bo turned serious and intertwined his fingers as he spoke.

"How's the investigation going? Found who did it yet?"

The chief slowly shook his head.

"The case has its ups and downs. We managed to weed out a few suspects, but nothing more."

Bo nodded.

"I see."

"So, down to the reason behind my visit."

The chief leaned forward in his seat and cleared his throat as he spoke.

"One of our suspects was seen around these parts earlier today."

Bo gasped.

"Wow. Has he been caught yet?"

Chief Danvers tilted his head to the side as he examined Bo's expression. Bo felt nervous as the chief silently watched him. Eventually, the chief spoke up.

"Well, sort of. Did you see anything?"

Bo slowly shook his head.

"No, not really. Why?"

The chief went on.

"Well, the suspect's car was parked in front of your trailer. Do you know Steve Harris?"

Bo's eyes widened, and he slowly nodded. He could feel his heart straining against his chest, and it made him feel very uncomfortable. Bo calmed himself and responded.

"Steve? Steve was here earlier today."

Bo uncrossed his leg and sat straight as the chief replied.

"Well, we think he had something to do with the three robberies that happened a few weeks ago."

Bo feigned further shock as he replied.

"And he seemed like such a sweet boy."

The chief nodded and went on.

"Some of my guys caught up to him and tried to bring him in for questioning. Unfortunately, it didn't work out."

Bo lifted a single eyebrow as he responded.

"What happened?"

"He ran. My men gave chase and ended up shooting the poor kid."

Bo could picture Steve panicking and fleeing before getting shot. It wasn't a pretty picture.

"That sounds horrible."

The chief nodded in agreement.

"It is. I didn't even get a chance to talk to him. What a mess."

Bo held his hand against his head.

"And he was in here, practically begging me for a job."

Chief Danvers looked up.

"So, he did work for you?"

Bo looked up thoughtfully and slowly nodded his head.

"Yeah, sort of. Howard down at the hardware store recommended him when my power washer was acting up. He did a great job with the machine, so I paid him extra to power wash some concrete at a building site."

Bo stroked his chin and kept his gaze fixed on the ceiling as he thought back to the event.

"I've hired him to do a few odd jobs here and there."

The chief silently stared at Bo. He thought through the tale and nodded to himself.

"So, he wasn't a full-time employee?"

Bo firmly shook his head and laughed.

"Oh, God, no. Steve was a good kid, but he was pretty slow and inefficient. What a normal guy would have completed in four hours usually took Steve about six to seven hours. He was inefficient but thorough and cheap. Good enough for the occasional job, but not good enough to be on the payroll."

The chief quietly listened to Bo's story and nodded.

"Alright, then. Did you see what he was driving?"

Bo smiled and nodded.

"See it? I heard it. All the way from the bottom of the road."

Bo shook his head.

"You should have seen my surprise when it came to a stop in my driveway. I heard it again when he stormed out of here, angry that I didn't have a job for him."

The chief nodded along.

"Did you take a good look at the car? What did it look like?"

Bo nodded.

"It was a unique shade of blue and had white stripes. That's all I remember."

Chief Danvers smiled and tapped the edge of his nose.

"That's the one."

Bo folded his hands and frowned.

"I wondered where he got the cash to afford the car but didn't read too much into it."

The chief's ears perked up, and he committed the statement to memory.

"So, you've never seen him in that car before?"

Bo nodded.

"Steve showed up in different vehicles whenever I had a job for him. But the cars were nothing special. If it wasn't a beat-up truck, it was a cruiser that was barely hanging on. You can understand my surprise."

Chief Danvers nodded in agreement.

"We were wondering the same thing. We've got a guy from St. Louis helping with the investigation."

Bo's ears perked up at that bit of information. He filed it away for later use.

"He was the one that found out about the car. From the info we gathered, it didn't make any sense. Steve shouldn't have been able to afford that car. I just wanted to have a little chat."

Bo spoke up.

"Not to be nosy, but you said you have a guy from St. Louis helping with the investigation?"

Nathaniel nodded.

"Yeah. Major Crimes up in St. Louis sent us a guy fresh out of school. He's been accommodating so far. It's especially wonderful seeing as we are shorthanded. We lost a guy after the last budget cuts."

Bo nodded along and responded.

"Have I seen him around?"

Nathaniel shrugged.

"The kid isn't that hard to pick out in a crowd. He always has a suit on and doesn't know how to loosen up."

The chief laughed heartily.

"A couple more weeks here ought to loosen him up. Hopefully, this case doesn't last that long."

Bo thoughtfully stroked his chin as he digested the information offered by Chief Danvers. He snapped his fingers and smiled.

"I just realized something. That's what the old-timers were talking about the other day."

The chief looked up and furrowed his eyebrows.

"What do you mean?"

Bo leaned forward and laughed nervously as he recounted his tale.

CHAPTER 19

BEARER OF BAD NEWS

"While I was down at the café, I overheard the old-timers saying something about soup."

Bo chuckled and shook his head.

"I could not for the life of me figure out what they were on about. They were probably saying suit, not soup."

Bo and Chief Danvers shared a laugh, and Bo went on.

"It didn't make any sense until now. Glad I got that off my mind."

The chief shook his head and smiled.

"You know how those old-timers slur their words. It's hard to make out what the heck they're saying half the time."

The chief shrugged.

"What can you do?"

Chief Danvers turned to the clock in the room and slowly rose to his full height. Bo beat him to the punch and was up in an instant. The chief smiled at Bo as they walked towards the door.

"Well, sorry I had to come down and ask you about all of this. I'm just making sure we cover all our bases."

Bo shook his head and smiled.

"There's no need to apologize. You're just doing your job."

The chief extended his hand, and Bo took it in a firm handshake.

"That's sad to hear what happened to Steve. He was such a nice kid. I can't believe it ended like that."

Bo sighed and shook his head.

"Maybe I should have given him the job. He might still be alive."

The chief slowly shook his head.

"Don't do that. Don't blame yourself. It wasn't your fault."

Bo felt a knot of guilt in the pit of his stomach. He ignored the feeling and went on.

"If only he was eager regularly. I might have given him more work. He seemed so determined to get a job today."

The chief stroked his chin and filed that information away for later use.

"That's something to consider."

The chief paused at the door.

"Anyway, thank you for your time. I'm sorry if I interrupted your call."

He pulled open the door and stepped out. Bo held the door open and smiled as he responded.

"Oh, that? Don't worry about it. I was talking to an agent about closing a deal by the end of the week. I can always call him back."

The chief nodded and walked to his car.

"I see. You're always working hard. Keep it up."

Chief Danvers waved through his window as he started the car and pulled out of the driveway. Bo waved and smiled as he watched the chief drive out to the main road. Bo continued to wave until he was confident the car was out of his sight. Bo's smile fell, and he stroked his chin.

"What a mess."

His mind kicked into overdrive as he considered the

different outcomes of the situation he was faced with. Frustrated by his thoughts, he emptied his mind and walked back into the trailer, content to slam the door behind him.

⊕

Doug sat in his chair, frowning at the TV as he enjoyed a beer. He had a lot on his mind, but didn't want to think about any of it. He tried to drown out his thoughts with the sounds of prime-time cable. At a point, it started working as a show came on that earned his interest.

Doug's concentration was broken when a knock came on his door. He looked up, startled and annoyed.

"The kid wouldn't knock like that. I wonder who that is."

Doug wasn't in the mood to receive any guests but answered anyway.

"Maybe he forgot his keys. He was in a hurry to leave after all."

Doug opened up the door and frowned at the faces he noticed. Andy and Jay stood, their expressions blank as they observed Doug. The silence that followed lasted for a split second and was broken by Andy.

"Doug, may we have a word with you?"

Doug eyed both men and frowned.

"What's this about?"

Andy went on.

"Please, it's important that we talk to you."

Jay interjected.

"Can we come in? It's about your nephew, Steve."

Steve's name caught Doug's interest.

"He isn't here if that's what this is about."

Andy slowly shook his head.

"It's not. So, can we come in?"

Doug's head told him not to let them in, but he realized it would seem suspicious if he didn't. Doug nodded and stepped aside, holding the door open for Andy and Jay to walk in.

Doug led the lawmen to his living room and created space on the couch for them to sit.

"Can I interest either of you in a beer?"

Andy shook his head.

"No, thank you."

Doug shrugged and gulped his.

"More for me. Well, get straight to the point. What do you have to say?"

Andy's face reflected his internal turmoil. He didn't know how to tell Doug that he had lost his nephew. Andy figured the best thing to do was to just come out and say it.

"About Steve. He got stopped a few hours ago and tried to run away. In the process of giving chase, he was gunned down. The kid didn't make it."

The hardness in Doug's eyes vanished entirely. He could not believe what he was hearing. Doug crushed the beer can he had in hand and flung it towards the kitchen, angrily.

"Damn it, kid!"

He glared at his clenched fists as he fought to keep his emotions in check. Doug had not been expecting anyone to get shot, much less his nephew. While he felt a sense of loss, he was still cautious and carefully eyed the officers in front of him.

"What was he pulled over for?"

Andy responded.

"It was about the car he was driving. No papers or plates. Did you know about it?"

Doug slowly shook his head.

"Not really, no. I wouldn't have let the kid go out without plates if I did."

Andy nodded.

"Good point. When was the last time you saw him?"

Doug stroked his chin as he considered the question.

"The other day. You two came by earlier on. Steve returned that evening with some loud car. Disturbed half the neighborhood."

Andy nodded and whipped out his notepad before responding.

"Did he say where he had been?"

Andy noted down a few things as he listened to Doug's reply.

"At the casino. The kid had been gone for a few days. My guess is he spent the weekend there and ran back once he was out of luck. Steve was only here for about an hour or two before he left again."

Jay took over the questioning.

"Did Steve tell you where he was headed or what he was going to do?"

Doug scratched his chin and considered the question.

"Something about finding work to do. Steve seemed pretty excited about it before he ran out of the door."

Doug frowned sadly.

"I haven't seen him since then."

Doug sighed and leaned back in his seat. He ran his fingers through his hair and turned his attention to the ceiling. Andy spoke up.

"Sorry. I'm sure this is hard for you."

Doug nodded and leaned forward.

"I'll be fine. Go ahead."

Andy went on.

"The car you spoke about. Did you see what it looked like?"

Doug furrowed his eyebrows as he considered his response.

"It was pretty dark by the time he got back. It looked blue from the small glimpse I could get, but I can't be sure. I didn't see the model or the make. Heck, I could barely see the color."

Andy scribbled that down and nodded to himself before going on.

"Did he tell you where he got it from?"

Doug firmly shook his head.

"It didn't come up, and I didn't ask."

Andy spoke up.

"You have to agree that it was a rather expensive car. Did you ask him where he got the money to afford it?"

Doug shook his head.

"The kid's an adult. It was none of my business, and I'm not the type to pry. Besides, we didn't talk much in the little time he stopped here."

Jay looked up and lifted a single eyebrow.

"Little time? You said he was here for two hours. That seems like enough time for a discussion to me."

Doug frowned as he responded.

"True, it felt shorter. As I said, he didn't say much. He spent most of that time in the garage before eventually heading out again."

Doug shifted uncomfortably in his seat.

"I'm sorry we're asking so many questions. We just want to make sure we understand everything. Can you tell us what Steve has been up to lately?"

Doug shrugged and casually responded.

"The kid stayed here sometimes, but he would be in and out occasionally. When he was around, we would work on car engines together."

Doug thought back to his time with Steve and grit his teeth as he suppressed his anger.

"Sometimes, he would disappear. He'd be gone for a day or two, looking for work. You'd think he was hard working from the way he looked for jobs."

Doug shook his head and chuckled drily. Jay interjected.

"Speaking of work, what line of work are you into?"

Doug furrowed his eyebrows as he replied.

"I work at the junkyard and do the occasional engine repair work out of my garage. Why do you ask?"

Andy shook his head.

"It doesn't matter. Anyway, I'm sure you have some emotions to sort through. So, we'll leave you to it."

Andy and Jay got up and walked toward the door. Andy paused in his tracks and turned.

"Look, for what it's worth, I'm sorry for your loss. He seemed like a good kid."

Doug remained in his seat as they walked towards the exit. Andy turned to gaze at Doug one last time before shutting the door, effectively plunging the room into darkness. Silence fell over the living room, and Doug didn't move so much as an inch as he continued to glare at the floor. He clenched his fists and gritted his teeth.

⊕

Andy's cruiser came to a halt in front of the police department. He shut off the engine and sighed as he palmed his face.

"Well, that was draining."

Jay nodded in agreement.

"You could say that again."

The pair stepped out of the car and entered the building as they conversed with one another. Andy and Jay walked into the bullpen side by side and continued to discuss the case as they approached Andy's desk. The chief's office door was open at the end of the room, and he noticed as they walked in.

"Andy, Jay. Come in here for a second."

Andy and Jay answered the chief's call and sat across from him. Chief Danvers leaned back in his seat and carefully observed the pair as he spoke up.

"So, how did things go with Doug? How did he take the news?"

Andy furrowed his eyebrows.

"He was calm but unsettled. I noticed some turmoil on his face."

Chief Danvers leaned back in his seat and nodded.

"Were you able to get any new information from him?" Andy responded.

"Well, from what he told us, he hasn't seen much of Steve lately. We didn't get any useful information out of him."

Jay spoke up.

"From the look of his place, he doesn't have any money on him. The house was in a sorry state. If he was part of the robbery, he isn't spending any of the money."

Andy nodded in agreement.

"I noticed that also. It still doesn't clear him, though. We need more information."

The chief spoke up.

"Did he give you any hints that he knew where Steve and the car were?"

Andy frowned.

"He said Steve showed up yesterday evening, and while Doug admitted to hearing the vehicle, he said he didn't see much of it."

"So, he wasn't able to describe it?"

Andy shook his head.

"All he knew was the color, not much else."

The chief digested the information handed to him by both officers as their meeting wore on.

CHAPTER 20

WORTH LOOKING INTO

The conversation continued with a question from Andy.

"How about Bo? Were you able to get anything out of him?"

The chief shrugged.

"Bo confirmed that Steve came over looking for work earlier that day."

Andy perked up.

"So, Steve worked for Bo?"

Chief Danvers shook his head.

"Well, not really. Bo hired Steve to do the occasional job, but Steve wasn't on his payroll. He said that Steve left his office angry because he didn't have a job for him."

Jay listened carefully to the chief and asked a question.

"What did Bo say about the car?"

The chief leaned back in his seat and responded.

"He said Steve was one to drive different junkers to work. He described seeing Steve in different vehicles, all in bad shape, and was surprised by the hot rod. His expression seemed genuine when he responded."

Andy stroked his chin as he considered the information offered by Chief Danvers.

"So, what do you think about Bo? What was your read on him?"

The chief fell silent for a long moment as he organized his thoughts.

"When I walked in on Bo, he was on the phone with one of his agents about closing a contract. It felt like business as usual down there."

He intertwined his fingers and went on.

"I think Steve turned to Bo as his last resort when he realized how bad his situation was. It's understandable given what Bo had done for the kid. I'm not suspicious of him. So, until further evidence comes to light, he isn't a suspect."

Andy nodded along to the chief's explanation and spoke up once he was done.

"Well, chief. If you think Bo is innocent, then I'll take your word for it."

Chief Danvers nodded.

"He's been a model citizen for as long as I've known him. It didn't look like he was having money problems, and he doesn't strike me as the time to rob if otherwise."

Jay leaned forward in his seat and furrowed his eyebrows.

"So, are we writing off Steve's visit as a coincidence?"

The chief nodded.

"Until some hard evidence comes into play against him, he's clear."

The chief rifled through the papers on his table and produced a small notebook.

"My search wasn't a total waste, though. I came across a name that's worth looking into."

Andy sighed and nodded.

"Sure, Chief. At this point, any lead would be helpful. All we have is one guy, and we still aren't sure he did it."

The chief cleared his throat and began.

"So, when Jay brought up Steve and his uncle, I decided to look into everyone associated with the pair. I came across the name of Phil Sexton."

Andy was intrigued.

"Who's that."

"Back in the day, Doug and Steve's dad had several run-ins with the law. Phil Sexton was one of their associates. Phil lives in Twin City now. That isn't too far from here, and there's a likelihood that they stayed in touch. It's worth looking into."

Jay glared as he collected all the info being thrown out by the chief.

"So, Steve, Doug, and Phil. Do you think those are our three guys?"

The chief shrugged and shook his head.

"I'm not sure. But there is a connection. As I said, it's worth a shot."

Andy nodded as he rose from his seat.

"Good enough for me."

He turned to Jay and smiled.

"So, want to keep riding with me? What do you say?"

Jay nodded and got up.

"Definitely. Let's go."

Andy tipped his hat to the chief as he walked out. The pair exited the room side by side and headed out to do some more investigating.

⊕

The chief was nice enough to hand Phil's address over to Andy. It wasn't too long of a drive to Twin City, the rundown part of town across the railroad tracks. The pair finally arrived at Phil's apartment building. Andy stared at the place as his car came to a halt and whistled. He eyed the directions in his hand and frowned.

"Just as I thought. It doesn't say what apartment belongs

to Phil."

Andy got out of the cruiser, and so did Jay. The pair walked up to the entrance and noticed something off about the building. It was split down the middle and had two front doors. Jay spoke up.

"It looks like this place has two wings. Did the chief say what wing Phil lives in?"

Andy looked down at the writing once more and shook his head firmly.

"All I have here is a numbered address. It didn't specify whether or not it was A or B."

Jay and Phil eyed both entrances frustrated.

"So, what now?"

Andy walked up to one of the doors.

"You knock over there, and I'll knock here. Phil is bound to step out of one of the doors. If not, we'll ask after him."

Jay nodded in agreement as he walked to his half of the building. Andy counted to three with his fingers and the pair rapped against the doors in unison. Silence fell over the neighborhood after their knocking, and neither could hear sounds of movement in the house.

Andy knocked again and pressed his ears to the door.

"Silence."

He noticed a small window at the side of the door and peered in. Andy spied a small hallway with a set of stairs leading to the second floor. The floor was covered by a ratty mat with holes in it, and all the doors on the ground floor were closed.

Jay knocked again on his end, and there was no reply. He leaned over the railing and managed to get a view of the backyard. The lawn at the back was littered with junk and looked like it hadn't been mowed in ages—still, no sign of any tenants. Jay turned to Andy and spoke up.

"Nothing back there but turning grass and some old junk."

Andy frowned and folded his arms.

"Nothing through the faded blinds, either. The place looks pretty empty."

Andy turned to Jay and went on.

"Let's take a lap around this place and see if we can spot any open windows or people."

Andy wrapped around from the right and Jay from the left. Andy kept his eyes peeled for signs of life. He looked through some of the windows he walked by, but the story remained the same. The pair met up in the backyard, and Andy scratched his head.

"Still, no one. What about your end?"

Jay folded his hands and shook his head.

"Same here. Let's head back to the front."

Andy and Jay walked to the entrance and stepped off of the porch just as a sedan appeared at the head of the street. The car looked worse for wear and might have been black at some point. The car drove by Andy and parked across the street. Jay nudged his partner and gestured towards the vehicle.

"Is that our guy?"

Andy shrugged.

"The chief didn't say anything about the kind of car he drives. Let's wait and see."

Andy and Jay watched as a middle-aged man stepped out of the vehicle and walked in their direction with groceries in hand. He didn't pay them much heed and would have walked right by if Andy hadn't called his attention.

"Excuse me?"

The man paused in his tracks and looked up with piercing eyes.

"Yes?"

Andy stepped closer to the man and went on.

"Are you Phil Sexton?"

Jay recognized the eyes and hair and immediately knew they had their guy. Phil's eyes darted from Andy to Jay in initial confusion, but he quickly calmed down.

"Yes, that's me."

Jay walked up and smiled.

"That's great. We would like to talk to you about an old friend of yours. Doug Harris. Does the name ring a bell?"

Phil nodded.

"I know Doug. I see him at AA meetings every once in a while."

Jay nodded.

"And when was the last time you saw him?"

Phil stroked his chin as he carefully considered the question.

"Now that you mention it. It has been a while since Doug has attended a meeting. I haven't seen him in weeks."

Phil maintained a calm exterior while Jay analyzed him.

"I see. What did you guys talk about?"

Phil laughed and slowly shook his head.

"Sobriety. What else are you meant to talk about at an Alcoholics Anonymous meeting?"

Jay shrugged.

"I don't know. Love, life, his nephew Steve, maybe."

Phil shook his head once more.

"Steve isn't much of a drinker. He doesn't have a problem as far as I know. Why would he come up?"

Andy interjected.

"Well, he could have talked to you about the new car Steve got. That seems like an interesting topic of conversation."

Phil maintained a passive look while he responded.

"Steve got a car? There's so much to catch up on. I guess I'll ask Doug the next time I see him. As I said, he hasn't been there in a long time."

Phil eyed both of the men.

"Besides, why would a car matter to me?"

Jay shrugged.

"Maybe because it got him gunned down yesterday?"

Phil's shock was apparent and unhidden. He clenched his

fists and gritted his teeth. Jay took note of this.

"Does the news bother you?"

Phil turned on Jay.

"Of course it does. The kid was trying to do right, always out there looking for steady work. You just told me a good kid died. Why wouldn't I be upset?"

Jay softened slightly and nodded.

"So, you have no idea where Steve got the money for the car?"

Phil took a deep breath and sighed.

"As I said, I haven't seen or talked to either Doug or Steve in a while. Heck, I didn't even know he got a car. I can't believe the kid's gone."

Jay nodded.

"So, let me get this straight. You haven't made contact with either of them, say, in the last two weeks?"

Phil furrowed his eyebrows as he considered the question.

"It's closer to a month, actually. Several AA meetings have gone by without Doug attending."

Andy spoke up.

"And you haven't spoken to Doug outside of AA?"

Phil firmly shook his head.

"Doug wasn't the type to be buddy-buddy. Neither am I, to be honest."

Andy and Jay shared a brief look, and Andy turned back to Phil.

"Alright, then. If you come across any information related to Steve's car or you hear something from Doug, make sure to give either Jay or me a call. Steamboat Police Department. You know the number?"

Phil nodded, and the pair turned to leave.

"Awesome. I look forward to your call. Thank you for your time."

Phil watched Andy and Jay walk towards a police cruiser. He watched as they got into the car and then turned to leave.

Andy and Jay settled into the vehicle.

"Did he seem a bit nervous to you?"

Andy nodded.

"Did you notice his alligator skin boots?"

Jay slowly shook his head.

"I didn't think to look at his feet."

Andy nodded understandingly.

"The only reason it drew my attention is that I have a pair exactly like those. Those shoes are four hundred and eight dollars. Where does a guy living in this area get that kind of money?"

Jay frowned.

"His car also looks like it has seen better days. I doubt the car itself is that expensive."

Jay chuckled, and Andy smiled. Andy turned his attention to the building and watched as Phil returned.

"So, what do you think?"

Jay frowned and stroked his chin as he considered the question.

"There's a lot to consider here. The chief was right about looking into him."

Andy nodded in agreement.

"I say we keep a close eye on Phil and see what he does next. I'm not buying his story about not having spoken to Doug in weeks."

Andy started up the car, and Jay kept his eyes fixed on the apartment as they drove away.

CHAPTER 21

EMERGENCY MEETING

Doug sat in the living room; the place dimly illuminated by a single lamp as he stewed. He had a lot on his mind, but there were pressing matters that needed attending to.

"I can mourn for the kid later."

Doug eyed his landline and picked up the receiver. He dialed a number and waited as the phone rang. After three rings, the recipient picked up.

"Bo speaking. Might I ask who is calling?"

Doug sank into his seat and glared off into the darkness as he replied.

"No name. But it's me."

Doug was banking on the fact that Bo would recognize his voice. Luckily, he did.

"How did you get this number?"

Doug replied.

"You have at least five signs around town. It wasn't that hard."

Bo sighed over the line, and silence prevailed for a short while.

"What do you want?"

Doug peered out his window as he replied.

"We need to meet."

Doug could feel the reluctance drifting through the receiver.

"Are you sure?"

Doug nodded to no one in particular.

"I wouldn't be calling if it wasn't urgent."

Bo sighed once more and fell silent again before speaking.

"Fine."

Doug followed up.

"It needs to be soon."

Without offering any more details, he hung up the phone.

⊕

"It's through this way," Bo said.

A door opened up at the head of the stairs, shedding light on the otherwise dark room that lay beyond. Phil peered through the darkness and tried to make out any shapes but was unable to see anything.

"Are you sure it's safe down there?"

Bo nodded and took to the stairs.

"I'm positive. Mind your step."

Phil eyed the dark passage cautiously as Doug walked ahead of him. With Bo and Doug gone, Phil decided to follow. He was still wearing his new boots, and they made a satisfying clunk when they hit the wooden steps.

Phil eyed the passage behind them before shutting the door, and followed Doug and Bo down the steps. Bo expertly navigated his way through the room and came to a light switch. He flicked it on, chasing away the darkness and casting light on the scene.

Phil gasped in surprise as he eyed the tastefully decorated room. The exquisite furnishings were the star of the show, and the overall design was aesthetically pleasing. Doug let loose a soft whistle as he plopped down in one of the seats.

"This is quite a nice place you have here."

Phil nodded in agreement.

"The furniture looks amazing. Is this one of the places you worked on?"

Bo nodded and smiled.

"It took a while, mainly because I was uncertain about some of the design elements, but I'm satisfied with the final results."

The trio sat in silence for a brief moment and took in the calm atmosphere. Bo was the first to snap back to reality and cleared his throat.

"Right, on to pressing matters. We didn't come here to admire the drapes, did we? Did you bring what we discussed?"

Doug and Phil both held up satchels and gently placed them on the coffee table. Bo eyed the satchels and nodded.

"We can proceed, then."

He got up from the couch and walked forwards.

"Follow me."

The room was a lot larger than it initially seemed. Bo led his companions past a fully stocked bar and around a pool table. Doug eyed the drinks as they walked by, and Phil smiled at the pool table.

"This place is like a bunker. It's quite impressive."

Bo sighed.

"I built it to function as a storm shelter, not to hide from the police. But I guess this is the best place to talk without fear of being heard."

Phil smiled.

"Don't worry. It will go back to being a storm shelter once we've concluded our business."

Bo led the pair to a safe built into the wall.

"Is it in there?"

Bo nodded and walked up to the keypad. He typed in a

code and blocked the safe with his body. The keypad beeped in confirmation, and the safe door swung open, revealing a stash of valuable items. Among the items stashed away in the safe were four piles of cash.

"One stack per man. We were meant to be four here, but I guess it couldn't be helped."

The three men fell silent for a second as the weight of Steve's loss hit all of them at the same time. Doug clenched his fist and gritted his teeth.

"The damn kid just had to take a bullet!"

Doug shook his head and faced the money.

"I'm taking his cut."

Neither Bo nor Phil had any objections. Bo stepped aside and watched as Doug took what was rightfully his and stuffed it into the satchel he brought along. Doug made sure to do a rough count as he loaded up the money, and it took quite some time. Phil eyed the process and frowned.

"So, I got a visit from two guys earlier today. They were standing at my front door when I got back from buying groceries."

Doug paused after stuffing another collection of notes into his bag.

"It was probably the same guys that were at my place."

Bo was surprised by the news.

"Wait, you two were visited? Someone is looking into you?"

Doug nodded.

"One of them is officer Andy. We all know Andy. The second is some young guy in a suit. I haven't seen him around before."

Phil spoke up.

"He's from Major Cases Crimes up in St. Louis."

Doug turned to Phil and lifted a single eyebrow.

"How do you know that?"

Phil shrugged.

"Andy said so, right after he said to contact him if I learn something or remember anything."

Bo was clearly distressed. He paced on the spot and muttered to himself.

"I didn't think things were this bad. Do you think they suspect something? What a mess!"

Doug zipped up his satchel and glared at the floor.

"It doesn't matter."

Bo and Phil were surprised to hear that from Doug of all people. Bo was the first to respond.

"What do you mean 'it doesn't matter'? What if we get caught? All of this would have been a waste of time."

Doug slammed his fist into the nearby wall, and Bo fell silent.

"My nephew was killed, damn it! Compared to that, nothing else matters."

Doug got up and turned on the pair.

"I admit I didn't prepare myself for any casualties. I didn't think I would need to. This all started when that idiot bought that stupid car. Why the hell did he want a car so much?"

Doug deflated, and his anger turned to sadness.

"Anyway, I'm not sticking around to see what happens next. I'm taking my share and getting the hell out of here."

Bo tossed his hands into the air in exasperation.

"I don't believe this. Why did I get wrapped up in all of this?"

Bo laughed sardonically and shook his head.

"Now you plan on running and leaving the rest of us to face the consequences."

Doug settled further and sighed.

"Money makes us do desperate things, things we wouldn't think ourselves capable of doing."

Bo glared at Doug.

"Don't give me that larger-than-life bull crap."

He sighed and placed his thumb against his forehead.

"Whatever. The quicker I get rid of this money, the better. Out of sight, out of mind."

Phil interjected.

"Be careful about how you go about it. Remember, we aren't meant to spend any of it until the six-month period is up."

Bo turned on Phil with his rage.

"You know that. Yet, you walked in here with new boots. What's that all about?"

Doug looked up and nodded.

"You noticed as well? I was hoping it was some joke."

Doug grabbed the bag and double checked the zipper, then he stepped out of the way to allow Phil to get a crack at the safe. Phil walked up with his open satchel and reached for the next stack of cash.

"There's nothing wrong with my boots. They aren't flashy."

Bo shook his head slowly.

"They look pretty flashy to me. Both Doug and I noticed the second you walked in. So much for keeping a low profile."

Doug nodded in agreement.

"It's out of character. Did you wear expensive leather boots before the heist? We agreed to keep up appearances."

Doug took a deep breath and exhaled.

"Whatever. As long as you weren't wearing those when the lawmen visited you. That would be a disaster."

Phil paused and looked over his shoulder briefly. He then went back to loading his money into the satchel. Bo leaned against the nearby wall.

"While you guys were being visited by lawmen, I had the chief of police drop by my trailer the other day. It wasn't pleasant."

Doug looked up in shock.

"The chief dropped by your trailer?"

Bo nodded slowly.

"He was asking me about Steve. Someone must have spotted Steve when he dropped by my trailer."

Doug approached Bo and gripped him by the shoulders as he stared into his eyes.

"What did you say to him?"

Bo held his hand up in surrender.

"I didn't say anything, I swear."

Doug wouldn't hear it.

"I don't believe that for one second. What the hell did you say to my Steven? Did you push him to his death? Is this all your fault?"

Phil realized that the tension in the room was reaching a critical point. He stepped between the fighting pair and forced them apart. Phil kept a firm grasp on Doug and dragged him away from Bo.

"Calm down. You're getting unnecessarily agitated."

Doug relaxed slightly and dropped his tone.

"I want to know what he said to Steve. Maybe then I can understand why he had to die."

The anger in Doug's voice was replaced by sadness. Bo spoke up in a low voice.

"I didn't say anything to Steve. He dropped by my trailer and seemed to be agitated. He was asking me to put him on my payroll. Said he bought a car and needed an alibi for the money he spent."

Doug pushed Phil off and adjusted his shirt. He took a deep breath and eyed Bo.

"And what did you say to him?"

Bo leaned against the wall behind him. It was clear that he was tired of the situation.

"I told him I couldn't. It was clear that he was reaching. When I said no, he started begging me. It wasn't an easy call on my part, but I couldn't have helped without risking everything. I simply don't have that much money tied to my business. It would look suspicious."

Doug frowned.

"Why was the kid so adamant about it?"

Bo sighed and ran his fingers through his hair.

"He was going on about how he would be able to clear the car he got. Heck, I didn't even know what car he was talking about until he stormed out of my office. The engine was loud enough to wake up the whole neighborhood."

Phil nodded, and Doug fell silent. Bo pushed off the wall and stood straight.

"It sounds like we could all use a drink to calm down."

Doug's eyes lit up, and he nodded.

"Or six. What have you got in the bar?"

Bo walked forward and signaled for Doug to follow him.

"I'll show you."

Phil looked up from his task and sighed.

"I'll join you guys in a minute. Let me just finish off here."

Phil walked out with his satchel in hand and noticed Doug and Bo silently sharing a drink. He eyed the alcohol and smiled.

"I haven't had a drink in seven years."

Phil set down the satchel by the bar and sat on a stool.

"If there's any time to break my sobriety streak, it's now. I'll have what he's having."

Doug poured himself another shot of whiskey and glared off into the distance. Bo nodded.

"Coming right up."

CHAPTER 22

FINAL FAREWELL

Bo walked up to the bar as Phil took a seat.

"Pappy Van Winkle it is."

Bo got a fresh glass, made Phil a neat then set the glass on the bar top in front of him. Phil swirled the contents of his glass and smiled at the liquid.

"Let's see if it tastes as good as I heard."

Phil took a sip, and his eyes shut as he savored the flavor.

"So, what do you think? Is it as good as you heard?"

Phil gulped down the drink and sighed.

"Better. That's worth screwing up my chips."

Doug lifted his glass and smiled.

"A couple of chips can't hold a candle to a good drink."

Phil gulped down the rest of his drink and coughed.

"Another, with ice this time."

Bo played bartender, dishing out the drinks while the trio talking. Doug mellowed considerably and tendered an apology to Bo.

"I'm sorry I snapped earlier."

Bo shook his head and smiled.

"There's no need to apologize. I understand."

Doug frowned at his drink as he went on.

"I just don't know how to feel with Steve gone. It's a lot to take in."

Bo poured another drink and took a sip before responding.

"Steve was a good kid. He was a little over-energetic, but so are most guys his age."

Doug smiled and shook his head.

"He was also a little stupid. I honestly thought he was ready, but I guess I was wrong."

Doug sighed and downed his drink.

"Life moves on."

Phil nodded in agreement.

"It helps to have all this cash."

They continued to drink and talk until Phil called it to a close.

"Alright, guys. I think I've had enough to make up for all the years that I've missed."

He chuckled and shook his head.

"Any more, and I'll get shit-faced."

Doug nodded in agreement.

"I think we should call it quits while we can still walk on our own two feet."

Bo returned the drinks to their rightful places on the shelf behind him and wiped down the counter.

"The bar is closed for business. It was a pleasure serving you good folks."

Doug smiled.

"That was a strong hand you poured with the good stuff."

Bo smiled.

"It's a hobby. I like to take out the top-shelf whiskey now and then."

His smile deflated a bit, and he went on.

"Well, gentlemen. I guess this is the end. I can't say it's been a pleasure, but it wasn't all that bad. Honestly, I hope we never meet again."

Doug nodded in agreement.

"Well said. Don't expect any postcards. The only time you might see me is if I get caught. Otherwise, I'm avoiding this place like the plague."

Phil chuckled and shook his head.

"I'm still not sure how to move forward."

He turned to Bo.

"I don't mean to pry, but what do you plan on doing with your share."

Bo shook his head.

"I don't mind answering. As I said, I had my reasons for taking part in this mess. The real estate market has been volatile for a while now, and my business was close to going under."

Bo clenched his fists under the bar as he went on.

"I couldn't let all my hard work go to waste. So, when Doug approached me with his offer, I was more than ready to jump on it."

Doug grumbled.

"Even though you did turn me down the first time."

Bo chuckled and shook his head.

"No hard feelings. Anyway, everything will change this Friday. I'm about to close on another project. Once the capital rolls in, I'll be able to mix in some of the money in the safe. No one is going to ask where an extra twenty or forty thousand dollars came from. Even if they do, I could just say it was the cash deposit or down payment."

Phil nodded along with Bo's explanation.

"So, what will you do with the money until then?"

Bo turned to his safe and smiled.

"As you've seen, the safe down here isn't easy to find. I'll just keep the money in there until I need it."

Phil nodded and smiled.

"You really thought this through, huh?"

Bo nodded.

"I never go into any venture unprepared."

Doug spoke up.

"As I said, Bo had as much of a reason to go into this as we did. Hell, he has more on the line if this goes south. There's no reason not to trust him."

Phil nodded in agreement.

"I see that now."

Bo nodded.

"Plus, I'm not that much better off than you guys."

Phil held his hands up and shook his head.

"Whoa, let's not get carried away. Let's not pretend we aren't sitting at your private bar enjoying expensive bottles of whiskey."

Bo shook his head.

"Do you know that land that my trailer sits on?"

Phil nodded.

"Well, that's where all my money is. I poured everything I own into securing it. But if the county doesn't follow through with its plan for Highway 121 down to Highway 8, I might be screwed."

Doug chuckled and shook his head.

"He has rich people problems."

Phil had a lost look in his eyes, and Bo decided to explain better.

"Alright, so the trailer and lot are just a small part of the property. I own two hundred acres spanning across the hillside and including the dense forest around that area. That's a lot of development for me to do by myself."

Bo's eyes twinkled as he went on.

"But, if the county gets involved like they plan to, that may not be a problem. They would have to level that hill to finish Highway 121. And if I have Ray's Tree Service take down a lot of the greenery, I'm left with a pretty flat piece of land that spans about two thousand linear feet."

Phil's eyes widened, and he let loose a soft whistle.

"That's a lot of land. It's also a huge gamble."

He shook his head and chuckled.

"Doug was right, rich people problems."

Bo sighed and nodded.

"Yeah, you're right. The risk is immense. But if the county makes good on their promise, then the reward would be worth it. That's why I decided to join in on this crazy project of yours. The money could help cushion the blow if the deal doesn't follow through."

Bo shook his head.

"At least now I don't have to worry about being homeless."

He smiled and went on.

"Heck, if everything works out, I can retire and never have to work again."

Doug eyed the clock over the bar and frowned.

"Well, I think we've spent too much time here as is. So, I'm going to call it a day."

Doug slowly got up and tapped Phil on the shoulder.

"Now you know why Bo is in this with us. Are you satisfied?"

Phil nodded and shot up from his seat.

"Definitely."

Doug turned.

"Good. Let's head out while we still have daylight."

Phil reached across the counter and offered Bo a handshake. It was the first time the latter had seen any form of respect in the former's eyes. Bo took his hand, and Phil patted him on the shoulders.

"You're a good man. It's a pity you had to get wrapped up in all of this. But at least I understand why now."

Doug grabbed his satchel from under his seat and looked over his shoulder as he walked away.

"Thanks for the drinks, and of course, the money. I doubt we will ever see each other again. So, take care of yourself."

Bo nodded as he walked out from behind the bar.

"It was a pleasure doing business with you. Safe travels."

Doug turned to Phil and went on.

"Are you ready to leave?"

Phil grabbed his satchel and nodded as he got up.

"Let's get going."

Bo escorted the pair through the basement and up the stairs. He shut the door behind them, and it felt like they were exiting a dream. Reality returned when Doug opened the front door. He double-checked that the house wasn't being watched before stepping out.

"This is where we say goodbye."

Doug and Phil walked out of the entrance, and Bo firmly shut the door behind them. The silence that fell over the room was deafening. Bo took a moment to calm his mind before walking away.

⊕

Andy and Jay stood in front of Doug's home. Both seemed more than a little frustrated and silently watched the front door. Andy was the one to break the silence.

"Knock again. He's bound to be in there. If we don't get an answer, I'll check the garage."

Jay nodded and rapped against the metal storm doors, louder and for an extended time. He stopped when he heard the sound of footsteps on the other side of the door.

"I think that did it."

What followed was the latch being drawn back and the door slowly opening up. Doug glared at the two lawmen on his porch and grumbled as he stepped out.

"Oh, it's you two again. What do you want? I'm not exactly in the best mood right now."

Doug folded his arms and lifted a single eyebrow as he awaited a response. Andy paused and considered his next words carefully. He knew he needed to handle the situation delicately and proceeded to do so.

"The forensics team is done with Steve's body. We have him in the morgue, and you need to come down and identify him since you're his next of kin."

Doug grunted and shook his head.

"The kid hasn't been back since you told me he got shot. So, I'm guessing you have the right body. Now, if you'll excuse me."

Andy stopped the door from shutting and continued to speak.

"I'm going to have to insist that you follow us down to the station."

Doug glared at Andy but maintained a calm tone as he responded.

"And why is that?"

"In addition to identifying Steve's body, we need to ask you some questions."

Doug lifted his eyebrows.

"Questions? What for?"

Jay spoke up.

"Your nephew is dead. There's a lot about him that is still a mystery. You might be able to fill the blanks."

Andy nodded.

"Also, we would like to ask you a couple of questions concerning an incident that happened a few weeks ago. It's in your best interest to quietly follow us down to the station so we can sort this out."

Doug frowned as he responded.

"I want a lawyer, then."

Jay shook his head.

"That was quick."

He took over the coercion.

"We processed Steve's car and found a couple of note-worthy items in there. We would have asked Steve about them, but you know. So, since you're his next of kin, it only makes sense that we ask you instead."

Doug felt trapped. He wasn't sure how to respond. He decided to test the waters and figure out how serious his predicament was.

"And what if I say no?"

Andy sighed and shook his head.

"One of two things could happen."

He held up his index finger and went on.

"We could cuff you and drag you down to the station by force. In that scenario, we can only hold you for twenty-four hours before we have to let you go. But a lot could happen in that time."

Andy held up his middle finger and went on.

"Or, you could willingly follow us. We just need you to answer a couple of questions, and we'll let you go. It's as simple as that."

Andy let go of the screen door and tucked his fingers behind his belt.

"So, what will it be, Doug?"

Doug's eyes darted back and forth between Andy and Jay as he considered his next course of action. Being held for twenty-four hours didn't sit right with him, and he knew what he had to do.

"Fine, I'll go with you."

Andy smiled and nodded.

"That wasn't so hard, now was it?"

CHAPTER 23

QUESTIONING

Doug turned to leave.

"Where are you going?"

He paused in his tracks and sighed.

"To get dressed. Unless you want to take me down to the station looking like this."

Andy drew back and nodded.

"Fine."

Doug paused by the entrance and turned to Andy and Jay.

"I've agreed to follow you down to the station, but if you're planning on holding me, then I'm saying it right now. I want a lawyer."

Andy scratched the back of his head and sighed.

"Fair enough."

Doug nodded curtly and slammed the door in their face.

"He's got a bit of a temper."

Jay remarked as he and Andy descended the porch steps. Andy shrugged and walked up to his police car.

"I've seen worse. Let's just hope that he keeps to his word."

The pair waited for quite some time, but Doug eventually

emerged from his home and got into his car. He pulled out of his garage and pulled up beside the police car.

"Where are we headed?"

Andy started up his car.

"Follow us."

Andy pulled out of his parking spot and drove off down the street with Doug hot on his tail. Andy eyed the rearview mirror and furrowed his eyebrows as they made their way over to the police station.

"Keep a close eye on him. We wouldn't want him driving off."

Jay nodded and kept his eyes fixed on Doug's car. Doug eyed the officers ahead of him. He had no idea how bad the situation was, but he knew he needed to make a call.

"The problem is, I have no idea if those guys are watching me or not."

Doug frowned.

"If they see me making a phone call, it'll look a lot more suspicious. They'll ask a lot more questions than I am ready to answer." Doug reached into his pocket without taking his eyes off of the road and retrieved his phone. He flipped it open and dialed a familiar number.

Doug set the phone on speaker mode and placed it between the two front seats. The phone rang for a few minutes without a response.

"Come on."

Soon the line clicked, and Doug knew he was through.

"Hey, it's me. Don't say a thing."

He kept both of his hands on the wheel and made sure to look ahead as he talked.

"Those pesky lawmen came to my house again today. This time, they insisted I follow them down to the station."

Doug was careful to use the bare minimum lip movement to avoid arousing suspicion from the other car.

"I'm on my way there right now. I have no idea where you

are or what you're doing. But I highly recommend you get rid of that money and disappear. Things are starting to heat up on this end, and you don't want to get caught in the crossfire. Trust me."

Doug hung up the phone and replaced it in his pocket without saying another word. The car in front of him continued without slowing, and he hoped they weren't onto him. Doug paid attention to the road as they continued on their journey.

Soon, a red brick building came into view, and he spotted the not-so-familiar sign of the Steamboat Police Department. Andy brought his car to a halt in front of the building and stepped out. He walked up to Doug, parked a few feet behind him, and leaned his head into the window.

"We're here. First, we'll pay a visit to the morgue so you can confirm Steve's identity. Then we'll have our little chat."

Doug nodded and stepped out of the car. He followed closely behind Andy and Jay as they walked into the building. The trio didn't pass that many people on their way to the morgue. Andy led the way to a room one floor below ground level.

Andy pushed open the steel double doors leading into a relatively cold room and walked to the center. Jay and Doug followed closely behind him, and they halted in front of a gurney. A body was sprawled out on the gurney, and over it was a white tarp.

Doug eyed the tarp warily. He wasn't looking forward to seeing what was below it.

"Do we really have to do this?"

Andy nodded.

"We need to be a hundred percent sure."

The doctor in charge of the morgue walked into the room with a clipboard in hand. He paused when he noticed the three standing in front of the body.

"Andy. If you're here, then I assume this fine gentleman is

the uncle of the deceased?"

Andy nodded.

"We brought him to identify the body."

The mortician set down his clipboard on a table at the back of the room and returned to the gurney.

"Alright. The body didn't have that many cuts or bruises, so patching him up wasn't all that difficult."

The mortician gripped the edge of the white material and frowned.

"Are you sure you're ready?"

Doug furrowed his eyebrows as he stared down at the body.

"No, not really. But these two won't let me leave unless I do. So, we might as well get this over with."

The mortician nodded and slowly lifted the cloth over the body. Doug's breath caught in his throat as he stared down at the all too familiar face of Steve. His nephew looked a lot paler than usual, and his eyes were shut, but he could never mistake his brown hair and his slender facial features.

Doug remained silent for a while, and Andy chose to let him marinate without disturbance. After a while, Andy grew impatient and asked for an answer.

"So, is that Steve?"

Doug felt tears fighting to be freed at the back of his eyes. He blinked them back and turned away from the body as he responded.

"Yup, that's him, alright. He still looks as stubborn as ever. Even in death."

The mortician nodded and replaced the tarp over Steve's body. Andy walked up to Doug and placed a calm hand on his shoulder.

"Sorry, you had to go through that. I'm sure it wasn't easy."

Doug remained silent and nodded. Andy walked away and decided to give Doug a moment to deal with his emotions.

After staring off into the distance for a few minutes, Doug turned and nodded.

"Alright, I'm okay."

He returned to the gurney and stared down at the body.

"When can I get his body?"

The mortician returned.

"I just need to run a few more tests, and he's all yours."

Doug frowned.

"I need to call the rest of the family, I guess."

He sighed and looked up at Andy and Jay.

"I identified the body. Are you happy? Can I leave now?"

Andy steeled himself for the storm that was to follow.

"Look, I know this wasn't easy, but we still need to ask you some questions. It shouldn't take long. So, if you could just follow me, we can get this over with."

Doug turned and ran his fingers through his hair as he sighed. He looked over his shoulder at Andy and nodded.

"Fine. Lead the way."

Doug and Jay followed Andy through the building. They returned to the main floor and navigated through the different halls until they arrived at the bullpen. Doug took a moment to admire how tightly packed the office was. Andy led the way past all the cubicles and right into the chief's office.

"Right this way, Doug."

Doug nodded and walked by Andy. Andy held his hand out as Jay was about to walk in. He waited until Doug was out of earshot before speaking.

"It doesn't make sense for both of us to be here while one more suspect is at large."

Andy turned to Jay with a severe expression.

"I've got this handled. Can I trust you to find Phil and bring him in?"

Jay nodded and turned to leave. Andy watched him exit the room before stepping into the chief's office. Chief Danvers sat with his fingers intertwined as he observed Doug. Doug had no idea what to make of the man seated across from him, but he could tell that he meant business.

Chief Danvers leaned back in his seat as he spoke.

"Doug. Do you know who I am?"

Recognition reflected in Doug's eyes, and he nodded.

"Yeah, Chief Danvers, if I am not mistaken. But I didn't vote for ya."

The chief nodded and gestured towards Andy.

"You've already met Andy. Now that formalities are out of the way. What say we get right down to business?"

The chief pointed to a seat in front of his desk as he went on.

"Why don't you take a seat."

Doug kept his eyes peeled on the chief as he took a seat. He felt trapped with Andy behind him and the chief before him. Doug took a deep breath and calmed himself before they went on.

"I'm glad you accepted our invitation to come here today. I'm sure it was a difficult choice, given what happened to your nephew."

Doug grunted.

"You say it like I had a choice. Let's just get this over with."

Doug sighed.

"What do you want to know? I already told Andy over there everything I know. What other information could I possibly offer?"

The chief's expression remained passive as he responded.

"Well, we finished processing Steve's car and found a few interesting things scattered here and there. The most interesting piece of evidence we found was a couple of hundred-dollar bill bands that said Boatman's Bank."

Doug managed to hide his rage. Even in death, Steve still found a way to mess up. Chief Danvers tried to measure Doug's response to the news before going on.

"Would you happen to know anything about that?"

Doug slowly shook his head.

"Nope."

Nathaniel eyed Doug carefully, hoping to catch something from his facial expression.

"Are you familiar with the robberies that happened a few weeks ago?"

Doug slowly nodded.

"Yeah. It was all over the news. What of it?"

Chief Danvers leaned forward and rested his elbows on his table.

"Well, we have reason to believe that Steve was part of the party responsible for those robberies."

Doug snorted and chuckled.

"I'm sorry. Do you think Steve managed to pull off something like that? The kid could barely tie his shoes."

Nathaniel frowned and leaned back in his seat.

"Do I think he planned out the heist? No, I don't. But we have evidence that can place him at the scene of one of the three robberies. We suspect all three were conducted by the same group, a three-man crew at the very least. And we believe Steve was one of those three men."

Doug frowned and leaned back in his seat.

"Look, I've said my piece. I don't think there is anything else I can offer. We are done here, but if you plan to hold me further, I want a lawyer. I already told Andy this before we arrived."

Chief Danvers held up his hand.

"There's no need to get defensive. We're just having a little conversation."

He smiled as he went on.

"Look, the truth of the matter is, we found missing money bands in your nephew's suspiciously purchased car."

The chief leaned forward and fixed Doug with a calculated glance.

"Now, Steve lived with you. You two worked together. If

anyone could tell us anything about that car and the money, it's you. And you're trying to tell me you didn't know anything about it?"

Doug nodded firmly.

"I don't like repeating myself, Chief. Andy already asked me that same question. The kid didn't say anything about the car or the money."

Doug leaned forward in his seat.

"Look, I can't say much for my dead nephew. All I know is he was trying to be a good kid, and now he's dead. I can only speak for myself. So, unless you have a question for me that concerns me, I think this meeting is over."

CHAPTER 24

QUESTIONABLE CIRCUMSTANCES

Andy immediately swooped in to salvage the situation.

"Let's all calm down. We're adults. We can talk this out."

Andy turned to Doug.

"You've made a fair point. Let's leave Steve out of this for a moment and talk about you. Is that alright?"

Doug settled into his seat and nodded.

"Can you account for your location the weekend these robberies happened? Where were you?"

Doug grunted and shrugged.

"Hell, if I know. My memory isn't what it used to be. What weekend are you talking about exactly?"

Andy fought to remain patient as he responded.

"The robberies that happened two Saturdays ago. You should know, because it was all over the news."

Doug scratched the back of his head as he feigned ignorance.

"Could you be a bit more specific?"

Andy was at the end of his patience, and that was obvious from his facial expression. He fumed as he responded.

"Where were you on the morning of the parade? You should at least know when the parade started that Saturday."

Doug dug into his ear with his pinky as he thought up a response. He blew on the gunk that came out and smiled.

"I spend most Saturday mornings in bed or on the couch. It depends on where I fall asleep the previous night."

Doug shrugged.

"I drink a lot on Fridays and end up hungover Saturday mornings. Once I recover from my hangover, I grab something to eat and head over to the garage to get some work done."

Andy nodded along with Doug's explanation and noted it down.

"Is that what you did on the Saturday in question?"

Doug shrugged and frowned.

"Sure, I guess. Look, I already told you that my memory isn't all that good. I narrated my usual Saturday mornings. What more do you want?"

The chief nodded and sighed.

"Alright, calm down. Let's get back to the main question; the money bands we found in Steve's car."

He fixed Doug with a searching glance as he went on.

"Now, you're certain you have no idea how the money got in Steve's car?"

Doug nodded firmly.

"As I said, the kid and I didn't talk much when he stopped by."

Doug ran his fingers through his hair and sighed.

"I already told you he was in a casino up in St. Louis for most of the weekend. I can't say he got the money from there for sure, but it seems pretty likely."

Andy looked up with a glint in his eyes.

"You didn't mention St. Louis before."

Doug flared up and whirled on Andy.

"Well, what other casinos could he have gone to? We don't have any casinos in Steamboat, and I doubt he went all the way to Caruthersville or even Tunica for a weekend."

Doug's nostrils flared as he spoke.

"It's not like the kid could have gone to Vegas either. I talk, and you nitpick my words. I stay silent, and you ask me to talk. There's no winning with you, is there?"

The chief held up his hands and once again reigned in the argument.

"Relax, Doug. Andy is just trying to get all the facts straight. You aren't under attack."

Doug turned on the chief and relaxed his grip before settling into his seat.

"It sure felt like it."

The chief nodded.

"Look. We've managed to dig up some evidence and build a narrative, but there are still some annoying holes in the story that need to be filled."

The chief gestured towards Doug and went on.

"That's what we have you here for. We invited you here to my office so we could talk. We didn't toss you into the can. So, please, relax."

Doug took a deep breath and calmed down.

"Alright, alright. Look, I want to help. That's why I decided to come here. But I don't think I can. I don't have the answers you're looking for."

Doug turned from Andy to the chief as he went on.

"You want to know where the money bands in the car came from, but I don't know. You want to know how Steve bought the car, but I don't know that either. I have told you everything I do know. If that isn't enough, then I can't help anymore."

The chief turned from Doug to Andy and sighed.

"Fine. I hear you."

Nathaniel reached into his top desk drawer and retrieved a pen.

"You mentioned that your memory isn't all that strong.

Well, if you do remember what you did that weekend, don't hesitate to give us a call."

Chief Danvers slid over his notepad and handed Doug a pen.

"Also, if anything comes up in the near future, we will call you instead of coming all the way to your place. Does that sound better?"

Doug took the pen and nodded.

"Sure."

Doug eyed the pad and spoke up.

"What do you want me to put down?"

Chief Danvers leaned forward in his seat as he responded.

"Your phone number. So we can reach you if any more questions do come up."

Doug eyed the paper and nodded. He scribbled a set of digits and slammed the pen into the pad as he sharply rose from his seat.

"Is that all? Can I leave now?"

Nathaniel picked up the note pad and nodded. Doug paused and frowned.

"So, when can I get Steve's body?"

Nathaniel interlocked his fingers as he responded.

"The mortician just needs to run a few more tests. We'll send his body over to Frank's Funeral Home once we're done."

Nathaniel held up the note pad and nodded.

"I'll call you the second the body is in their possession."

Doug nodded.

"Isn't there some doctor or someone who examines the body before processing?"

The chief nodded back.

"Only in a high dollar TV show, not little old Steamboat."

Doug stood up and turned to leave. He paused at the entrance and shot the chief a cold stare before walking out of the door. Silence fell over the room in Doug's absence. Both Andy and the chief took a moment to process all the information they had managed to pry out of their suspect.

Andy looked up from his musings and eyed the notepad sitting on the table.

"Do you think that number is real?"

Chief Danvers nodded.

"Doug struck me as a smart man. I doubt he would put down a fake number."

Nathaniel stabbed his index finger against the notepad and went on.

"Plus, this is a local line. He gave us his landline, not his cell."

Andy shot out of his seat and walked over to the chief's desk. He eyed the notepad in question and frowned.

"Damn."

⊕

Jay sat in his car, patiently watching the bank across the street. Hillsboro Bank was in the next town over about eight miles away. A lot more customers had been trooping to and from the bank in the weeks following the robberies, despite its distance from the center of town.

None of that concerned Jay. What caught his attention was the familiar vehicle parked in the lot right in front of the bank. So, he waited for the owner to come out. Jay watched the bank entrance closely, not wanting to miss his target.

A few minutes went by without any activity. Jay checked his watch and frowned. Suddenly, the front door opened, and out walked Phil. Jay smiled as he watched Phil walk over to his car. He took note of the satchel in Phil's hand and shook with anticipation.

"Andy needs to hear about this."

Jay reached into his pocket for his phone and dialed Andy as he watched Phil step into his car. The phone rang for a few seconds, and Andy answered.

"You'll never guess who I found?"

The response was quick.

"Phil? Did you spot him at his place?"

Jay shook his head as he responded.

"Not exactly. I'm parked in front of Hillsboro Bank as we speak. Phil just stepped out of the bank a few minutes ago carrying a rather suspicious satchel in hand."

Andy whistled.

"How did you find him?"

Jay leaned forward in his seat and eyed Phil closely.

"I was on my way to his place when I spotted his beat-up car parked in front of the bank. I doubt I would have been able to recognize it if he was driving some silver four-door sedan. You've got to love small town America."

Andy grunted.

"Keep him in your sights. I'm on my way to pick him up as we speak."

Jay nodded and replied.

"How did things go with Doug? Did he squeal?"

Andy sighed and replied.

"We couldn't get anything useful from him, but he was jumpy the entire time. Hopefully, Phil will be a bit more cooperative."

Jay watched Phil pull away from the bank and started up his car. He made sure to follow at a safe distance and kept the car within his sights the entire time.

"Phil is on the move."

Jay heard the sound of Andy's cruiser door shutting as he responded.

"Where are you now?"

Jay gazed out his window and looked for discernable landmarks.

"It looks like we're headed south on Highway 121. We're headed your way."

Andy smiled on the other side of the line as his cruiser roared to life.

"Perfect."

⊕

Phil sat in an empty room with his head in his hand. Aside from the chair he was seated in, two others were present, separated by a steel table with a notepad. The room was eerily silent and gave him enough time to collect his thoughts. Phil knew the situation was dire, but he decided to suck it up and fight his hardest to get things straightened out.

Andy and Jay watched Phil from the other side of the one-way glass.

"That was easier than I thought it would be."

Andy closely observed Phil and remained silent. Jay spoke up once more.

"Do you think he will talk?"

Andy eyed the suspect and shrugged.

"It won't be easy, but I guess we'll find out."

Andy and Jay walked into the room side by side. Andy sat across from Phil while Jay walked to the back of the room and leaned against the wall. Silence prevailed in the room as both sides collected their thoughts and prepared for a long mental battle.

Phil hadn't looked up at their entry, but he eventually raised his head and met Andy's stare.

"So, Phil. Could you tell us what you've been up to?"

Phil slowly shook his head.

"I'm not saying anything without a lawyer."

Jay smiled at the back of the room and spoke up.

"Why so quick to lawyer up? That makes us think you have something to hide. We just want to know what you've been up to."

Phil shook his head.

"I don't care. You can try all the tricks you want, but unless I see a lawyer in here, I'm not saying anything."

Jay was about to say something in reply, but Andy held up his hand.

"You want a lawyer? That's not a problem."

Andy turned to Jay and spoke in a loud voice.

"Jay. Please, get this man his public defender. But make sure to let the lawyer know that his new client has a lot to answer for. Like, where he got the seven thousand dollars in cash, we found on him at the time of his arrest."

Andy smiled in Phil's direction and went on.

"Also, let the lawyer know that there hasn't only been one, but three banks robbed in this area recently. We wouldn't want the man to walk in on this case blind, would we?"

Andy stroked his chin and went on.

"Lest I forget the fact that his new client does not have a strong alibi for the day those three banks were robbed. There's also the fact that his new client hangs out with questionable friends."

Andy turned to Jay.

"Are you getting all of this down? Also, am I missing anything?"

Phil looked ashen as he watched the exchange going on between the two lawmen. Jay shook his head.

"Nope. You hit the nail right on the head. Couldn't have said it better myself."

CHAPTER 25

FINAL MISTAKE

Phil, to his merit, remained silent through the entire exchange. Jay eyed him for a brief moment, then nodded as he headed for the door. Jay paused with his hands on the handle and gave Phil one last look. He noticed the stubbornness in his eyes and shrugged before turning to leave.

A few moments went by, and Andy emerged from the room with a smile on his face. He searched for Jay and found him having a cup of water in the break room. Jay was surprised to see Andy out of the interrogation room so fast.

"Why did you come out?"

Andy leaned against the kitchen counter and grinned smugly.

"You can go ahead and cancel that lawyer. His services won't be needed."

Jay snorted and shook his head.

"That's just as well. I never called one."

Andy lifted a single eyebrow as he responded.

"Why not?"

Jay shrugged.

"I'm new here. I don't know any of the public defenders or the procedure for calling one."

Andy chuckled and shook his head.

"Why didn't you ask the lady upfront?"

Jay shook his head.

"She isn't there. And I wasn't planning on bugging the chief if it wasn't important."

Jay set down his cup, and Andy asked another question.

"So, you've just been here all this time?"

Jay slowly shook his head.

"Not really. I checked with the lady at the front desk first. When I saw she wasn't there, I did a lap around the office, then stopped here to get a glass of water."

Jay smiled.

"It all worked out for the best, I guess."

Jay eyed the interrogation room and frowned.

"So, why did you want me to cancel the public defender?"

Andy gestured toward the room as he responded.

"Phil is writing down what he knows as we speak."

Jay smiled.

"So, our improv worked, after all?"

Andy laughed and shook his head.

"Not exactly. He still seemed a little stubborn. So, I listed out all his priors and stated that it wasn't looking good for him. I offered him a deal if he was willing to give me some information, and he jumped at it."

Jay smiled and nodded.

"Works every time. Did he say anything?"

Andy nodded.

"He claims he was the wheelman and nothing else. He also stated that Steve hooked him up with the job, but he has no idea who the third guy is."

Jay nodded.

"So, it was a team of three?"

Andy ran his fingers through his hair and sighed.

"He didn't specify. Phil isn't giving up much information."

Andy and Jay walked up to the one-way glass partition with a view of the interrogation room. They watched as Phil nervously scribbled away at the notepad Andy left him.

Jay thinks out loud.

"Do you think he's telling the truth?"

"No," Andy responded.

Jay whistled and turned to Andy.

"That was fast."

Andy nodded.

"Well, I don't think he's saying everything. That much is painfully obvious."

Jay leaned against the wall and nodded.

"Did he say anything else?"

Andy nodded.

"Phil said they only paid him ten thousand dollars to drive. The seven thousand we found on him is what is left of his cut, according to him."

Jay frowned.

"That doesn't seem like much compared to the amount we're looking for. Something doesn't add up. We need to get the third man in here so he can fill in the holes."

He ran his fingers through his hair and sighed.

"It's a shame what happened with Steve. He seemed like the type to squeal with enough coaxing."

Andy nodded.

"We'll need to make do with what we have."

Jay stroked his chin as he went over the information offered by Phil.

"Phil tied Steve to the robbery, which he admitted to being a part of. That should give us enough to get a search warrant for Doug's place. Since Steve lived there."

Andy nodded.

"I was thinking the same thing. I also want to know who Steve was in contact with in the days leading up to the robbery. There's probably a clue in there somewhere. If what Phil said is right, then we might be able to catch the third person that way."

Andy turned and was about to walk away when Jay tapped him on the shoulder.

"You're leaving? What about Phil?"

Andy turned to stare at Phil and smiled.

"What's he going to do? Stab himself in the neck with a pen? He's safer here than anywhere else. We should have enough time to do some investigating."

Andy and Jay walked towards the central part of the station side by side. Andy broke off and stepped into the evidence room while Jay waited for him in the bullpen. Andy returned shortly after and reclined at his desk with a phone in hand. Jay eyed the old phone in Andy's clutches and frowned.

"Please, tell me that isn't your phone. I haven't seen a flip phone since I was a little boy. Do people still use those?"

Andy smiled and nodded.

"Not everyone can afford smartphones. Anyway, this isn't mine. It's Phil's."

Jay's smile deflated as he realized the gravity of the situation.

"Is that what you went into processing for?"

Andy nodded.

"I want to find out who he has been in contact with. We might be able to find out who his last accomplice is."

Jay frowned.

"Can we do that?"

Andy smiled mischievously.

"This is where you get free on-the-job training. So let's not worry about the technicalities."

Jay walked closer and eyed the phone suspiciously.

"Have you seen any names you recognize?"

Andy frowned.

"That's the thing. Phil didn't save the numbers with

names. So, there's no telling."

Jay was intrigued by that.

"Not even one?"

Andy shook his head.

"I've been scrolling since I got it out of the evidence locker. Still, nothing."

Andy sighed and held the phone away as he thought of what to do. Jay spoke up.

"So, what's the move here?"

Andy tapped his chin as he thought of a solution to their problem. His eyes suddenly lit up, and he drew the phone closer.

"Did you think of something?"

Andy nodded.

"I'm going to send out messages to some of the numbers here and see if I get a response."

Jay frowned.

"You think that'll work?"

Andy nodded.

"One of these contacts is bound to respond. It's a simple matter of waiting."

Andy frowned.

"So, he really didn't save any of these numbers?"

Andy nodded and handed the phone over to Jay.

Jay whistled softly as he scrolled through the empty, strange contact list.

"Even little kids save numbers with names. This is a first."

He handed the phone back to Andy.

"I really hope someone responds. I'm interested to see who Phil has been talking to."

Andy shook his head. He turned and got up from his seat.

"Well, I think we've given Phil enough time to sort through his thoughts. Let's go see what he has for us."

Andy walked out of the bullpen with Jay hot on his tail. The pair returned to the interrogation room and stared down Phil, who quietly sat in his chair. Andy sat across from him, and Jay took his place at the back of the room.

Andy smiled at Phil, but the latter kept his eyes fixed on the notepad. Andy picked up the notepad and carefully went through everything Phil had written down.

"I see."

Andy set down the notepad and stared down Phil.

"Is there anything else you would like to add?"

Phil finally looked up and glared at Andy.

"I've written down everything I'm willing to say. I'm not saying anything else."

Andy sighed and massaged the bridge of his nose with his thumb and forefinger.

"You know we have your phone, right?"

Phil grunted.

"And? What of it?"

Andy smiled mischievously and leaned forward.

"Well, you see Jay over there?"

Jay looked up from his notepad and stared in Andy's direction.

"He's a big wig from St. Louis. We noticed you don't keep track of your contacts. So, he had a genius idea. We messaged the recently contacted numbers. We're awaiting a response as we speak."

Jay was completely surprised by the turn the conversation had taken. But not as surprised as Phil. His jaw dropped, and he repeatedly shook his head.

"That cannot be legal. Isn't that invasion of privacy? You can't do that."

Jay caught on to what Andy was scheming and smiled mischievously.

"Sure, I can. I just did. You wouldn't believe all the power we have up in the big city compared to little old Steamboat."

Phil groaned and leaned back in his seat.

"This isn't right. We had a deal, and I kept up to my half of the agreement. I declared on paper that I took part in the robberies. What else do you want from me?"

Andy crossed his legs over the table and rested his head against his hand.

"I want names. Aside from you and Steve, who else was involved in this little scheme? How many people took part in the heist? And most importantly, where is the rest of the money?"

Phil rested his face in his palm as he responded.

"I told you, I don't know. It's standard for a crew to keep the driver in the dark for this specific reason. How can I tell you what I don't know?"

Phil leaned forward.

"I was paid upfront, and that was it. I haven't heard from them since then, and I sure as hell have no idea where the rest of the money is."

Silence hung heavy after Phil concluded his tirade. Andy remained calm and didn't allude to his suspicions.

"So, you never went into any of the banks?"

Phil looked to be at the end of his rope. He looked up with a tired expression and responded.

"I..."

Phil's response was cut off by an annoying buzzing sound that seemed to come from Andy's pocket. He smiled.

"Well, would you look at that?"

⊕

Bo was having a good day. He got up at the crack of dawn and headed down to his job trailer to get some work done. There was just one day to go, and he would be able to close on his next project.

"I wonder what I'll do with the rest of the money."

He spent most of the morning outlining his plan for the extra cash sitting in his safe at home. He had no idea that something unfortunate was heading his way. Everything flipped when he received the first message.

"That might be the agent."

Bo picked up the phone and scrolled through his messages. He noticed a message from Phil and paused with his finger hovered over the icon.

"I wonder what he could want."

Phil wasn't one to send a text message. Bo's curiosity overwhelmed his sense of caution, and he opened the message. The contents were pretty distressing.

"Looks like Phil's in trouble."

Bo dropped the phone on his desk and leaned back in his seat as he considered what to do. Phil had asked that he call back, but he wasn't sure he wanted any part of what was going on.

"I've done my part already. Why should I risk myself for his sake?"

Bo sighed and grabbed his head. He thought of Phil desperately in need of help and couldn't bring himself to ignore the message.

"I should at least find out what's going on."

Bo picked up his cell and opened Phil's unsaved contact number. His finger hovered over the call icon indecisively, and he couldn't decide whether or not to go through with it.

"Screw it. If he's in trouble, I need to know what's going on."

Bo dialed Phil and waited as the phone rang. The ringing went on for quite some time, and the anticipation built up to a worrying level.

"Come on. Pick up."

Eventually, Bo heard a click, then silence.

"Phil, are you there?"

No response came through, and he continued.

"I got your messages. What's wrong, man? Where's Doug? Phil?"

A voice Bo didn't recognize responded. "This isn't Phil."

CHAPTER 26

JAIL CELL REFLECTION

The line went dead; the second Andy spoke up, and silence hung heavy in the room. He and Jay shared a look as they tried to make sense of what had just happened. Phil seemed somewhat nervous, understandably so. He had no idea what to make of the situation and hoped that Bo would be smart enough to lie low.

Andy turned to Phil and spoke up.

"Who was that?"

Phil took a deep breath and steadied himself. He put on a cocky smile and shrugged.

"No idea."

He realized that neither Andy nor Jay immediately recognized the voice and hoped it would stay that way. Andy was about to question him further, but Jay approached him and whispered into his ear.

"We've already pushed this too far. We should return the phone to the evidence locker and work with what we have."

Andy eyed Phil menacingly and sighed.

"Fine."

He leaned forward and frowned.

"I'll ask one last time. Is there anything else you would like to add to your statement?"

Phil firmly shook his head, and Andy leaned back.

"Alright, then. Jay, you know what to do."

Jay walked up to Phil and cuffed him. He walked him out of the room and left Andy to his thoughts. Andy stared at Phil's phone, willing an answer to pop up on the screen. He thought back to the voice that called and couldn't shake the feeling that it sounded familiar.

"I've heard that voice before. But where?"

Andy got up and walked out of the interrogation room. He sauntered to his desk and plopped down as he continued to ponder the case. Jay returned and approached Andy's desk.

"I put Phil in the holding cell."

Jay pulled up a chair and plopped down next to Andy.

"He isn't going anywhere."

Andy nodded but remained silent, piquing Jay's curiosity.

"A penny for your thoughts?"

Andy looked up and sighed.

"I've been trying to remember where I've heard that voice before."

He grabbed a pen on his desk and absent-mindedly clicked it against his desk as he tried to conjure up a memory. The answer evaded him, and he sighed exasperatedly. Jay spoke up.

"We've learned a lot today."

Andy nodded.

"We should bring the chief up to date."

Jay turned to the chief's office as he rose from his seat.

"He should still be in."

The pair approached the office side by side, and Andy knocked on the door.

"Chief, are you in there?"

Nathaniel's chair creaked as he sat up.

"Yeah. Come in."

The pair walked in just as Nathaniel was putting away some papers. The chief leaned back in his seat and sighed.

"So, how are things going out there?"

Andy sat before the chief, and Jay hung back.

"Jay and I were able to get Phil in here. You should know that we caught him red-handed with stolen cash on his person. It took a little work, but we managed to talk him into spilling."

Chief Danvers leaned forward, eager to hear the rest of the story.

"Did he give up his accomplices?"

Andy sighed and shook his head.

"Phil insists that he was only the driver, but that he didn't know the other crew member."

Chief Danvers lifted a single eyebrow.

"Do we believe him?"

Andy frowned.

"It's hard to tell if he's telling the truth, but my gut tells me he is hiding something. I just don't know what exactly."

Nathaniel fell silent as he processed the information being handed to him.

"What about the money?"

Andy ran his fingers through his hair as he responded.

"That's another thing. We only caught Phil with seven thousand dollars. His story suggests he was only paid ten thousand since all he did was drive. We asked him what the crew did with the rest of the money, but he wasn't able to offer any explanation."

Chief Danvers rapped his fingers against the top of his desk.

"Where did you find him again?"

Jay spoke up.

"I spotted his car parked in front of the Hillsboro Bank. I watched the place for a couple of minutes before he came out with cash in hand."

Chief Danvers nodded and smiled.

"We should head back there and see if we can find any more of the money."

Andy stroked his chin.

"That sounds like a great idea. We'll get right on it."

He turned to the chief and went on.

"Phil also confirmed Steve as one of the thieves. He said Steve hooked him up with the job."

Nathaniel maintained a blank expression as he considered that piece of information.

"So, Steve really was one of the robbers. That takes a load off my chest."

Jay nodded in agreement.

"I've been feeling kind of guilty about what happened. It helps to know that he was in on it."

Andy spoke up.

"With Phil's testimony, we should have enough to get a search warrant for Doug's place. Steve lived there, and the rest of the money may be stashed somewhere on the property."

Chief Danvers listened closely to everything Andy had to say before responding.

"I'll contact a local judge and see what I can do about that. You two will have to go to the courthouse once I've put in a good word."

He interlocked his fingers and rested his elbow on the desk.

"What else did you learn from Phil's statement?"

Andy shrugged.

"Nothing. All he gave away was his part to play in the heist and Steve as his link to the responsible party."

Andy and Jay shared a look before the former went on.

"We did, however, learn something interesting using unorthodox methods."

Chief Danvers noticed a shift in the atmosphere, and his

expression changed to match it.

"What methods?"

Andy mellowed slightly as he responded.

"I might have used Phil's phone to send out a couple of messages to his contacts."

Nathaniel's eyes widened.

"You went through his phone?"

The chief massaged the bridge of his nose as he went on.

"Tell me you at least found something useful."

Andy nodded.

"He didn't save his contacts with names, but one of them called back. I kept silent initially and let him speak. The person I talked to knew Phil by name and also mentioned Doug."

Nathaniel snapped his fingers.

"Were you able to recognize the voice?"

Andy slowly nodded.

"It sounded very familiar, but I can't quite place my finger on where I've heard it before."

Andy grabbed a pen and paper and penned down a string of numbers.

"This was the number."

Nathaniel turned to Jay.

"Do you think your guys up in St. Louis could help us with a line trace? I want to know who this number belongs to."

Jay picked up the paper and eyed the digits.

"Sure. I'll talk to them when we're done here."

Andy smiled.

"A line trace didn't even cross my mind, since we don't have the equipment for it down here. That's why you're the chief."

Nathaniel smiled despite the gravity of the situation.

"We will know who was on the other end of that call soon enough. So, where is Phil now?"

Jay responded.

"I took him down to the holding cell and tossed him in. He

didn't resist."

Nathaniel nodded.

"Very good. We have a lot to cover, but we've made good progress in the case. Good job."

He rattled off the list of tasks.

"The first thing we need to do is work on that warrant. I'll call the judge right now, and you should be able to get it before the day is up."

Jay nodded and spoke up.

"Tracing the line will only take a few minutes, but we won't get the results until tomorrow. Since it happened here in Jefferson County."

Chief Danvers nodded.

"We also need to check with the bank about the money. Those are the three top priority tasks currently. Everything else is secondary."

Jay and Andy nodded in agreement. Nathaniel turned to face the window behind him.

"Now that you're clear on your tasks let's get right to it. We don't have the time to dilly-dally."

Andy and Jay rose from their seats and saluted. Nathaniel Danvers kept his eyes fixed on the scenery before him. His mind was working frantically to try and make sense of the case.

"This has been going on for far too long. We still have so many unanswered questions."

Danvers hoped to bring the case to a close within the coming week.

"We have one of them. The rest will soon follow."

Nathaniel reached for his line and held the receiver up to his ear as he dialed. He was put through almost immediately.

"Yes, this is Chief Danvers from Steamboat PD. I would like to speak with the judge, please."

Nathaniel calmly waited for a response. Once the judge was on the phone, he smiled.

"Avery, it's been a long time. I hate to ask out of the blue, but I need a favor."

✠

Jay ushered Phil to the lower levels of the police station. Phil's hands were bound together, and he didn't resist as he was led to a holding cell. Jay took the handcuffs off of him, and he walked into the cell.

"Try and get some rest. You're going to be here a while."

With that said, Jay walked out of the room. Phil massaged his wrists and sighed as he eyed the three walls surrounding him. He spotted an old worn bench at the back of the room. Instead of laying down, he sat with his head leaning against the cold, concrete wall.

Phil shut his eyes and went over everything that had happened that day. Getting caught hadn't been part of his plan, but there he was, sitting on a worn wooden bench of a cell.

"Life's a bitch, I guess."

Phil looked up at the ceiling and frowned. It wasn't his first time in a cell, and while he tried his best to suppress the memory, he slowly closed his eyes and took a trip down memory lane.

✠

In the late '80s, Doug and Phil met at a car show in St. Louis. The pair hit it off almost immediately over their love of '60s era muscle cars and stayed in contact after the show. One thing that united them was their shared love of drinking. Phil would often drop by Doug's place with a six-pack in hand, and they would spend the rest of the evening enjoying a cold one while they talked about life.

One night, Doug surprised Phil with his thoughts.

"Do you ever think life could be better?"

Phil turned to his friend.

"Of course, I do. All the time. My current situation isn't exactly ideal."

Doug laughed and shook his head.

"Life can be hard. But it doesn't have to be like that."

Phil downed his beer and burped.

"What can you do? We just need to roll with the punches."

A twinkle appeared in Doug's eyes as he replied.

"Or we could do something about it."

Phil looked skeptical.

"Like what?"

Doug fell silent for a moment as he carefully considered his response.

"There's a bank on Murdoch Avenue, Carrollton Bank. Heard of it?"

Phil nodded silently and listened as Doug went on.

"Well, I walk by it every day after work. I observed the place closely and noticed points of entry. I watched the guard's interactions every day. I noticed they are only open for two hours on Saturdays, so only one guard is present and that's only if they're there at all. Initially, it started as a pastime, but the more I watched, the more I noticed."

Doug paused to take a sip of his drink.

"I collected all the information I was able to gather and thought to myself, 'What the hell am I supposed to do with this?'"

Doug chuckled darkly and shook his head.

"From that thought, a plan took form. I started to think of ways to get into the bank without raising that much attention. I wondered if it would be possible for me to walk into the vault and walk out with a ton of cash."

Phil's eyes doubled in size as he realized what Doug was referring to.

"You can't mean..."

Doug fixed him with a severe stare as he responded. "Yup. I'm talking about robbing Carrollton Bank."

CHAPTER 27

CANVASSING FOR EVIDENCE

Andy's car pulled up to the courthouse. He found a spot to park and stared at the building as he spoke.

"Here goes nothing. Let's head in."

Jay nodded from the passenger's seat, and the pair disembarked. There didn't seem to be that much activity in the building, and Andy was able to walk up to the front desk. A perky lady looked up and smiled.

"Welcome."

Alice returned her smile.

"Thank you. Officer Andy here to see the judge. Is she in?"

The lady nodded.

"Do you have an appointment?"

Andy turned to Jay and he shrugged. He turned back to the lady and replied.

"I'm not sure; maybe something under Chief Danvers?"

The lady scanned through a small book and clapped her hands together.

"I have Chief Danvers penciled in. Right this way, please."

The lady at the front desk led them to a waiting area right

in front of the Judge's office.

"The judge will be with you shortly. Let me know if you need anything while you wait."

With that said, she turned and walked away. Andy sat, a little nervous about speaking to the judge.

"Judge Cortez is known to be pretty strict. This won't be easy."

Jay eyed the door beside them and frowned.

"How will we know when she's ready for us?"

Andy's response was cut short by a loud voice.

"Come in, please."

Andy and Jay got up sharply and walked to the door. Andy cleared his throat and knocked. Once given confirmation, the pair walked into a rather large office. Both sides were flanked by large shelves and at the head of the room was a mahogany desk.

Judge Avery Cortez sat behind her desk, her eyes fixed on the books in front of her. She looked up as Andy walked in and smiled.

"You must be Andy."

Andy nodded nervously and walked forward with Jay in tow.

"It's an honor to meet you, Judge Cortez."

Avery took his hand in a firm shake, and she shook her head.

"No need to be so formal. Please, have a seat."

Andy and Jay did as they were told, and Avery sighed as she did the same.

"So, what is this I hear about a warrant?"

Andy sat up and cleared his throat.

"We are currently investigating a string of robberies that happened a couple of weeks ago. We have one of the suspects in our custody and might have a lead on another. The testimony of the man we have in custody ties another culprit to the property. We hope to find something useful by the time we're done searching for the place."

Judge Cortez nodded as she processed the information handed to her by Andy.

"I spoke to Nathaniel over the phone, and he said as much. That should be enough for me to issue a warrant, but I don't want this to end up being an innocent citizen. How sure are you that you'll find something on the property that will justify this search?"

Andy frowned. He and Jay shared an uncertain look, and Avery turned from one to the other.

"Well? I'm eager to hear your response."

Andy nervously rubbed the back of his head as he responded.

"We're about seventy percent sure something will turn up."

Judge Cortez frowned.

"A hundred percent certainty would have been nice."

Avery sighed and massaged her eyelids as she thought.

"Alright. I'll issue the warrant because Nathaniel asked me himself. But for the sake of keeping things neat and tidy, try not to overstep. Are we clear?"

Andy nodded firmly, and Avery got up to retrieve the warrant. She looked it over before giving it to Andy.

"Use it wisely. If that is all, you can leave."

Andy and Jay got up sharply.

"Thank you for your help, Judge Cortez."

Avery swatted away his thanks.

"There's no need to thank me. Give Chief Danvers my regards."

Andy and Jay walked out of the room one after the other. Jay gently shut the door behind him, and the pair sighed with relief.

"That wasn't as bad as I thought it would be."

Jay nodded in agreement.

"It was still pretty intense, though."

Jay eyed the warrant and scratched the top of his head. "Now, what?"

Andy looked down at the paper in his hand and smiled.

"Now, we return to the station. We'll let the chief know we got it and head over to Doug's place right after."

⊕

The drive back to the station was uneventful. Soon, Andy and Jay were walking up to Chief Danvers's office. The former knocked and spoke up.

"Chief. We're back from the courthouse."

The pair walked in, and the chief looked up from the paper he was reading.

"That was fast. Did you get the warrant?"

Andy held it up and smiled.

"Judge Cortez said to extend her regards. Jay and I figured we'd let you know before heading over to Doug's."

Nathaniel held up his index finger as he responded.

"Before you head out, we should try the number Doug gave us. We did say we would call if something came up."

Andy took a seat, and Jay remained standing as Chief Danvers made the call. The line rang for a few minutes, but there was no reply.

"No reply. I hope he didn't run off."

Andy frowned.

"There's only one way to find out, I guess."

He turned to Jay.

"Are you ready?"

Jay nodded.

"Let's get Doug in here."

The chief chipped in.

"Be careful. Also, take as many officers with you as you can. I want that entire property canvassed for clues."

Andy turned to leave as he responded. "Will do."

✤

Three police cruisers arrived in front of Doug's home. Andy and Jay stepped out of one, another officer out of a Steamboat PD of the other. Along with two deputies sent over by Sheriff Mitchel stepping out of the third.

"You guys wait here while we check if he's inside."

Jay eyed the rundown house and frowned.

"I don't see myself getting used to this place. I wonder how anyone could live here."

Andy shrugged and knocked on the door.

"Police Department, anyone home!"

There was no immediate response, and Andy grew worried with each passing second. He peeped through the windows but couldn't make out anything through the darkness beyond.

"Knock again, maybe?"

Andy knocked with more urgency.

"Police Department, anyone home, call out!"

But once again, there was no reply.

"I guess he really isn't in."

Andy frowned.

"I don't like this. What if Doug actually decided to run?"

Jay turned and eyed the garage.

"His car is still in here."

Andy shook his head.

"He works on old cars. It's possible he made off with a different vehicle."

Jay stroked his chin.

"How about we check around the house? There might be an open door somewhere."

Andy nodded in agreement.

"I'll go right. You go left."

Andy walked to the end of the porch and jumped down onto a soft patch of grass. He searched the yard for any signs of life and noticed nothing. Andy walked down the right side of the house followed by a deputy and took note of how rundown the place was.

"We can't say he didn't have any motive. He could move out of this dump with that kind of money."

All the windows were locked shut, and Andy didn't notice any other entryways. He met up with Jay at the back of the house along with the other officers from Steamboat. The group stared at the back door skeptically. Jay tried the handle, but it was locked. He knocked against it.

"Police Department, anyone home, call out!"

Again, there was no response.

"It looks like we aren't getting in here today."

Andy shrugged.

"Or we could force our way in. We do have a warrant."

The group returned to the front as they discussed what to do next. Jay was about to reply, but paused when he noticed something in the distance.

"Hey, isn't that?"

Andy looked up and squinted. He was able to make out the facial features as the figure drew closer.

"Well, well. It looks like Doug didn't run after all."

Another beater of Doug's pulled in to his house, his eyes fixed on the road as he tried to run through his thoughts. Doug was genuinely surprised when he ran into the police in front of his place. One of the deputies greeted him as he exited his vehicle. Andy and Jay approached from the side of the house.

"Hey, Doug. Long time no see."

Doug groaned when he realized who he was talking to.

"Not you again. What do you want this time?"

Andy held up a warrant, and Doug's eyes doubled in size.

"We would like to search for this place. Could you open up

the door?"

Doug yanked his hand free from the deputy trying to hold him and scowled.

"Why should I?"

Jay spoke up.

"Because if you don't, it'll be considered an obstruction of justice. We will still get the keys and search the place, but you won't like how we go about it."

Andy smiled mischievously.

"So, what will it be?"

Doug sighed and reached into his pocket for his keys. He walked to the front door and unlocked it. The other officers entered the house and immediately began to thoroughly search his place from top to bottom.

"Hey! Careful with that stuff. That's all I have."

Andy shook his head.

"If I were you, I would be more concerned about them finding something incriminating."

Doug maintained a blank expression as they continued digging around. After a few minutes, one of Mitchel's guys walked out from inside the house and showed Andy a standard band customarily used for holding money. Andy peered at the lettering.

"Boatman's Bank."

He clicked his tongue and produced a pair of handcuffs.

"How unfortunate. Doug Harris, you're under arrest for robbery. Anything you say can and will be used against you in a court of law. You have the right to an attorney. If you don't have one, one will be provided for you."

Doug kept silent and didn't struggle as he was cuffed. Andy handed him over to Jay and turned to the rest of the officers.

"Keep searching. There might be more evidence hidden somewhere."

With that said, Andy returned to his cruiser, and the trio drove away from Doug's house.

✦

Doug stared at the wall on the other side of the interrogation room with empty eyes. He didn't have the strength to feel nervous or scared. He just wanted the whole mess to be over and done with. Andy and Jay walked into the interrogation room. The former sat across from him while the latter watched from the back of the room.

Andy placed a notepad before him and a pen.

"So, is there anything you would like to say?"

Doug thought of everything that had happened in the days leading up to his arrest. He thought of Steve, and the pain in his expression was plain as day. He remained silent.

"Look, I didn't want to say this, but we have Phil in here, and he's facing the same charges you are. He cut a deal, and you can too. Tell us what you know, and we'll put in a good word with the judge."

Doug looked up and scoffed.

"Please. This ain't my first time dealing with the cops. I'm not that green."

He sighed and shook his head.

"That being said, I'm tired of all this. I just want to grieve in peace. Is that too much to ask for?"

Andy didn't reply, and Doug eventually spoke up.

"I was involved in the robbery, but I didn't do much. Steve was in charge of most of it, from bringing us together to choosing the targets. The kid surprised me."

Andy and Jay turned to each other in disbelief.

"Wait, you expect me to believe that Steve was the brains behind these robberies?"

Doug shrugged.

"Brains would be stretching it a bit. He gave us our tasks. It was as simple as that."

Andy leaned back in his seat, clearly shocked by the story he was hearing.

CHAPTER 28

HISTORY REPEATS ITSELF

Andy managed to hide his disbelief by clearing his throat.

"So, Steve was in charge? That's the story you're sticking with?"

Doug nodded.

"So, what part did you have to play in all of this?"

Doug scratched the bottom of his chin as he considered what to say.

"Well, I organized most of the equipment we used. Nothing harmful, some junk cars with a couple of road flares and audio wires."

Andy folded his hand over his chest as he replied.

"The reports say that there were two armed robbers. One with a gun and the other with a bomb strapped to his chest. Were you any of these two?"

Doug firmly shook his head and Andy sighed.

"How many people were in the crew?"

Doug scratched the top of his head and smiled.

"It's difficult to say. I don't remember much from that day."

Andy slammed his fists on the desk and glared at Doug.

"Stop fucking with us and start talking. You already fessed up to being part of the robbery. What would it take for you to tell us about what went down?"

Doug remained calm as he replied.

"Look, I've said my peace. I told you the role I had to play in the robbery and even went as far as giving you the person responsible for setting it up."

Andy shook his head.

"A person who is conveniently dead and can neither confirm nor deny your accusations."

Doug glared at Andy.

"It's not my fault that you shot him."

The anger in Doug's voice calmed Andy to an extent, and he sighed as he ran his fingers through his hair.

"Look, I'm not trying to be insensitive. I just need to know what happened that day in as much detail as possible."

Doug shrugged and kept his mouth shut. Andy could tell that he wasn't going to get any more information out of Doug and sighed as he rose from his seat.

"It's pretty late. We'll try this again tomorrow. For now, Jay here will escort you to where you're going to be sleeping for the night."

Jay walked up to Doug and firmly cuffed him. Doug got up and let Jay lead him out of the interrogation room. Andy was left to his thoughts for the second time that day. He was trying to find a link between Phil and Doug's stories and felt a lot was still unknown.

"What's clear is that they are both telling the same story. Either they are telling the truth, or they were prepared to get caught."

Andy leaned back in his seat and stared at the ceiling.

"This is a mess. It all began when Steve got shot."

He leaned forward in his seat and furrowed his eyebrows.

"Was it just a three-man crew, or are we missing someone? Hopefully, the line trace will give us the answer we need."

✣

Jay led Doug through the building and into the holding cell at the lower level. He unlocked it and escorted Doug in after undoing his cuffs.

"Try and get some rest. We have a lot to go over tomorrow."

Jay exited the room and silence fell. Doug stared off into his new temporary cinder block housing and sighed.

"It wouldn't be the first time I slept in somewhere so depressing."

"I hear ya."

Doug was surprised by the voice that replied to him.

"Who's there?"

"Who else could it be?"

Doug traced the source of the voice and realized there was a cell on the other end next to his. He cautiously walked forward and stared at the little bit of iron metal he could see, as a hand was reaching out. Doug relaxed considerably, squeezing his hand through the aged metal to his longtime friend.

"They said you were in here. I thought it was just a ploy on their part."

Doug frowned and stared off into the distance as he went on.

"I told you to get out as fast as you could. How did you get caught?"

Phil smiled sardonically, and as he stared at the floor.

"Let's just say I made a rookie mistake."

Doug grunted.

"It happens to the best of us. I can't say I blame you. This has been one huge mess since Steve died."

Phil spoke to Doug.

"You might want to watch what you say. They could have the cells tapped."

Doug shrugged.

"We have nothing to hide. We're already in here."

Phil heard his friend and could tell that he would talk a lot less freely moving forward.

"Don't beat yourself up about it."

Doug leaned his head against the cold cell wall as he continued to speak.

"We'll get through this. We've done it before, and we will do it again."

Phil smiled.

"I was just thinking about the last job we pulled, actually."

Doug laughed and shook his head.

"It was such a mess. I remember feeling like hot shit back then. Imagine my surprise when we got caught."

Doug got a faraway look in his eyes as he thought back to more challenging times.

⊕

Doug took a large swig of his beer and cleared the side of his lip.

"I'm talking about robbing Carrolton Bank."

Phil laughed initially and slowly shook his head.

"It looks like you've had a bit too much to drink, my friend."

Doug looked up with clear eyes, and Phil realized he wasn't joking.

"Are you crazy? Why would we rob a bank?"

Doug listened to the sound of traffic outside of his apartment as he replied.

"I'm tired of living in the shit hole while jumping from job to job, barely being able to make ends meet. I want to wake up and the greatest worry I have is what to have for breakfast, not whether or not I can afford breakfast."

Doug's shoulder slumped.

"Life is hard. But it doesn't have to be. All we need to do is pull off this one job, and we'll be set for a very long time. Imagine being able to afford what you want instead of just staring at it through the store window?"

Phil's expression slowly shifted from startled to intrigued. It was obvious that Doug's words were starting to win him over.

"But what if we get caught? I can't go to prison, man. I'm not built for that tough environment."

Doug smiled.

"If everything goes according to plan, we'll be sitting on a large pile of cash without a care in the world. Only one question, what kind of car do you want, red or blue. I've thought this out, and I really think we can pull this off."

Phil turned to the window.

"Did you say Carrolton Bank on Murdoch Avenue?"

Doug nodded.

"The very one."

Phil sighed.

"Let me think about it. I'll get back to you."

Doug held his beer up to his lips as he replied.

"Think long and hard about it. You wouldn't want to regret your choice in the end."

Phil nodded. The pair enjoyed the rest of their time together, and Phil left once he noticed the sun starting to set. He paused by the door and took one last look at Doug before leaving.

The next day, Phil walked up to the Carrolton Bank entrance and looked at it with a different pair of eyes. He saw everything from the way the cameras were angled to the security officer stationed by the door. He tried not to make it too obvious and walked up to the counter.

"Yes, I was wondering if I could open an account here."

The lovely lady at the front desk smiled at him and handed him a form. Phil used his time at the bank to fully case the place out. By the time he left, he had his answer.

Phil returned to Doug's place later that day and all but ran to his front door. He banged on it as hard as he could, raising Doug from sleep.

"Keep your pants on. I'll be out in a minute."

Doug forced himself out of bed and staggered to the front door. He stared at Phil through sleep-filled eyes as he spoke.

"What the hell? Do you want to break the door down?"

Phil took a moment to catch his breath as he gathered his thoughts. Doug kept silent and waited for a response. Once Phil had his breathing under control, he stood straight and spoke up.

"I'm in."

Doug smiled and stepped aside.

"Come in, then. We need to discuss our business venture."

Phil stepped in, and Doug firmly shut the door behind him.

A few weeks went by without anything noteworthy happening in St. Louis. But all of that changed one sunny Friday morning. A car pulled up to the bank's entrance a little after nine, but no one stepped out immediately. Doug turned to Phil.

"Are you ready?"

Phil took a deep breath and nodded.

"Yeah."

Doug stepped out of the vehicle and leaned his head through the window.

"Remember, keep the car parked on the other side of the alley and keep the engine running. We need to be able to get out of here the second I'm out of the bank."

Doug turned and dashed into the building. The bank was a lot less busy than usual, and Doug knew that. He had been studying the place for weeks and knew exactly what to do. The first thing Doug did was to draw his weapon and fire once into the ceiling. He then pointed it at the lone security officer by the door.

"Everyone, out here and on the ground, now."

The security officer kept Doug in sight as he bent over. One of the cashiers managed to hit the silent alarm under the counter before crawling out with her companions. Once Doug was sure everyone was accounted for, he forced a cashier to the back and grabbed as much cash from the safe as she could fit into his bag. Doug made sure to keep the main area in view the entire time, and no one tried to contradict his instructions. By the time she was done loading his bag, Doug walked over to her and smiled.

"That wasn't so bad, was it? Now, I'm going to leave. Count to a hundred, then get up."

With that said, Doug walked out of the rear entrance. Doug spotted something in his periphery and paused in his tracks. He hid behind a dumpster and watched as two police officers walked up to the getaway car and called out to Phil.

"Shit!"

Doug dashed down the alleyway and hid again, careful to watch the car as Phil continued to talk to the officers. To Doug's utter dismay, Phil was asked to step out of the car, and the police led him to their vehicle in handcuffs.

"I need to get out of here."

Doug could hear more sirens approaching and tried to lug the bag along as he ran. He could not get very far with how awkward it was and was forced to stash it in a nearby dumpster.

"It should still be here by the time I get back."

His load lightened, Doug eyed his surroundings and ran as fast as his legs could take him.

⌗

Snapback to reality, Doug smiled to himself despite the bitterness of his thoughts.

"We were so close. I should have known there would be some sort of silent alarm."

Phil frowned.

"I got off light because I was just the driver, and you were never found."

Doug leaned back and stared at the ceiling.

"As if all of that wasn't bad enough, some asshole found the money where I stashed it and returned it to the bank. All of that effort wasted."

Phil frowned.

"I swore I would never end up in jail again after that disaster."

Doug sensed the pain in his friend's words.

"We'll make it through this. I'm not running away this time."

Phil sighed.

"You stuck to the story?"

Doug nodded and said, "Yep and now we wait this out."

CHAPTER 29

LINE TRACE

Jay yawned as he walked into the office the next day. With two hot cups of coffee in hand, he walked up to Andy's station to see if he was around. Andy was at his desk, working over the case files, as Jay approached.

"You're at it early again?"

Andy looked up and smiled. Jay grabbed a cup of coffee and handed it to Andy. Andy sipped from the steaming dark liquid and sighed.

"This is good stuff."

He turned back to the file on his desk and frowned.

"We have two suspects in custody, but things are far from over."

Jay pulled up a seat and took a sip from his coffee.

"We still have no leads on the money, and there are holes in the story. Neither Doug nor Phil is willing to be cooperative, and aside from the two of them being involved, we don't know much else."

Andy leaned back in his seat and folded his arms.

"Don't I know it? I've been staring at the facts all night, but

I couldn't find out anything new."

Andy turned to Jay.

"What's the status on the trace?"

Jay grabbed his bag and pulled out a notebook.

"That reminds me. I got the results early this morning. But I think we need to talk to the chief about this first."

Andy frowned.

"And why is that?"

Jay did not offer a reply. Instead, he handed Andy the book he had in hand and watched as he read through its contents. Andy's eyes doubled in size, and he looked up at Jay.

"Are you sure about this result?"

Jay nodded.

"Major Case Crimes doesn't joke about information. You can be sure that the trace was a hundred percent accurate."

Andy slammed the book on his desk and groaned as he leaned back in his seat.

"No wonder the voice sounded familiar."

Jay chose to remain silent while Andy processed his thoughts. He got up from his chair and grabbed the notebook.

"You're right. We need to talk to the chief about this. Come on."

Jay followed closely behind Andy as they approached Chief Danvers's office. Andy knocked on the door and walked in.

"Chief, are you there?"

Nathaniel Danvers looked up from the paperwork on his desk. He set down his pen and leaned back in his seat as Andy and Jay walked into the room. Andy remained standing and placed Jay's notebook on the chief's desk.

"Sorry to disturb you, but you're going to want to see this."

Andy piqued the chief's interest, and he picked up the notebook.

"What's this all about?"

Nathaniel read through the notebook and frowned slightly.

"What is this?"

Jay was the one to offer a response.

"The line trace results came in earlier this morning. That is the line registered to the number you handed to me."

Nathaniel Danvers stared at the book once more and sighed as he returned it to his desk. He got up from his seat and turned to face the window.

"And you're sure about the results?"

Jay nodded.

"One hundred percent, sir."

Nathaniel remained silent and observed the scenery outside his window.

"And I was so sure he was innocent."

He sighed one last time and returned to his seat.

"There's nothing to it, then. Bring him in for questioning."

Andy saluted.

"Will do, sir."

Nathaniel turned to Andy.

"Did you call the Hillsboro Bank?"

Andy nodded.

"I tried, but I couldn't get through to anyone important. Jay and I will have to go down there ourselves if we want to get anything done."

Chief Danvers nodded as he picked up his pen.

"Alright, then. Get right to it."

Andy nodded and turned to leave with Jay on his tail. Nathaniel Danvers set down his pen when the pair were gone and stared off into the distance.

"What the hell has he gotten himself into?"

⊕

Bo tossed and turned in his bed that morning, unable to fall asleep. He had woken with a start early that morning and didn't end up getting much sleep. Bo rolled out of bed and sighed.

"I might as well start my day."

It had been that way since the phone call he had made the previous day. He didn't recognize the voice that answered the phone, but one thing was sure.

"That wasn't Phil."

Bo had no way of telling who answered his call, and he had been on edge since the fiasco. That day, he had decided to close off from work early. It felt like every car he drove by was following him on his way home, and he couldn't get rid of the sickening suspicion that he was being watched.

Bo shook his head and glared at his feet.

"Why am I so tense? It's not like I offered my name. There's no way I've been found out. I just need to lie low and move on with life as usual."

Bo got ready in record time that morning and stood before a full-length mirror, ready to face the new day.

"Time to close another contract."

He took a deep breath and stepped out of his home. Bo pulled up to his work trailer after a quick drive and shut off his truck's engine as he stared at the trailer. He quickly got out of his truck and walked through the front door. Bo sighed with relief once he was safely behind his desk and prepared to receive his agent and client. After preparing for a few minutes, a knock came on the door, and he got up to answer it. Bo smiled at the pair and gestured for them to come in. The trio sat around his table and discussed the project.

"I've got to say that I am proud of the way the house turned out."

The client nodded in agreement.

"My wife loves it. You really did a great job."

Bo chuckled light-heartedly and rubbed the back of his head.

"It was a team effort."

He clapped his hands together and smiled.

"Right, then. Now that the formalities are out of the way

let's get down to business."

Bo leaned forward in his seat and set down some blueprints.

"Now, we just concluded the project, so I need to go over some of the extra costs incurred, and we can finalize on payment."

The client nodded, and Bo was about to follow up when a knock came on his door. He looked up, a bit surprised by the occurrence.

"Umm, were you expecting anyone else?"

They both shook their heads.

"My wife decided to stay back and check out the house."

Bo got up from his seat and walked over to the door. He opened it up and came face to face with a police officer and a man in a suit. Bo's heart rate went up, but he forced himself to smile.

"Umm, hi. How can I help you?"

The officer walked forward and responded.

"Are you Bo?"

Bo nodded.

"Yes, I am."

"I'm going to need to ask you to come with us down to the station for questioning."

Bo turned and peered into his trailer. He could tell that the client heard all of that and held up a finger to the officer.

"Alright. Give me a moment."

Bo returned to his visitors.

"Sorry to cut our meeting short, but apparently, they need me down at the police station."

Bo smiled and shook his head.

"I'm sure it's just something simple. How about we reschedule for tomorrow? I'll call you later?"

The client and agent nodded as they rose from their seats. Bo escorted the pair out of the trailer and watched them drive off. He turned to the police officer and spoke up.

"What did you say you need me for at the station?"

The officer walked forward and responded.

"We would just like to ask you a few questions. I'm sorry, I didn't know you had company. This should only take a couple of minutes, and you can be back here in good time."

Bo ran his fingers through his hair and sighed.

"Fine."

He got into the back of the cruiser, and the trio drove off.

⊕

Bo sat silently in the interrogation room. He knew he exuded nervousness and tried to bring his emotions under control. Andy and Jay watched him fidget from the other side of the one-way glass. Andy tried to read Bo and could tell he was nervous. Jay stared at him and frowned.

"He doesn't strike me as the type of guy to rob a bank. Look at his clothes and his watch."

Andy nodded.

"Bo runs a successful construction firm. Everyone knows him, and he's well-liked. Which is why I don't get why he would be connected to Phil."

Jay got up and approached the door.

"Well, that's what we're here to find out."

The chief walked up to the pair, and Jay paused with his hand on the door handle.

"Chief Danvers."

Nathaniel peered into the interrogation room and frowned.

"I'll take it over from here."

Andy and Jay shared a look. The latter nodded and stepped back.

"Alright, sir."

Chief Danvers walked into the interrogation room and sat across from Bo. He ran his fingers through his hair and sighed.

"Hey, Bo. How've you been?"

Bo relaxed slightly when he spotted the chief. He forced a smile as he replied.

"Things have been pretty hectic with me closing on a deal and all. I was a little surprised to get asked to come down here."

The chief rapped his fingers against the metal desk as he considered his response.

"Well, you're here for a good reason, I can assure you that. I just need to confirm a few things, then you'll be free to go."

Bo nodded.

"Ask away."

The chief leaned forward.

"Did you receive any strange calls yesterday?"

Bo was unable to hide his shock at the question. He slowly nodded.

"I did, in fact. How did you know?"

Chief Danvers leaned back in his seat and folded his arms.

"My men called a random number from the phone of a suspect we are currently investigating, and it happened to be yours."

Bo nodded along.

"Are you talking about Phil?"

Chief Danvers raised a single eyebrow.

"You know Phil?"

Bo nervously twiddled his thumbs under the desk as he replied.

"Roundabout yeah. I met him a few days after Steve died. He seemed pretty torn up about Steve's death and wanted to know what the kid was like in his final moments."

Chief Danvers fixed Bo with a searching glance. He eyed his mannerisms and his facial spasms. Aside from a little nervousness, he couldn't tell whether or not Bo was telling the truth.

"Is that all there is to your relationship with Phil?"

Bo nodded slowly.

"I was a bit surprised by the call. I thought someone was using his phone or something."

Bo laughed nervously, and the chief intertwined his fingers as he tried to figure out what to do next.

"Listen, Bo. These guys are not good people. They are responsible for so much loss. The money taken from those banks has still not been recovered."

Nathaniel leaned forward, and his expression was softer than usual.

"If you got mixed up in all of this somehow, talk to me. Let me help you. But own up to it."

A small tremor set in, and Bo was on the verge of cracking. The sincerity behind the chief's words caught him off-guard, but he quickly recovered.

"Look, I was trying to help Phil come to terms with Steve's death. I was the last person to see the kid before he passed. I was trying to fill in the blanks for someone who just lost a person close to them. That's the way I understood it. So, if there's any way I can help bring closure for his friend, I'll try. That's really all of it."

Silence fell over the room as Nathaniel continued to stare at Bo. He finally got up and turned to leave. The chief paused by the door and spoke.

"If that's your story, then I guess we're done here."

With that said, he walked out of the room and firmly shut the door behind him.

CHAPTER 30

HIDDEN LOOT

Chief Danvers walked out of the interrogation room, and his exit was watched by Andy and Jay. The pair stood silently, waiting for their commander to give an order. Nathaniel paced in front of the one-way glass and kept his eyes fixed on Bo. Jay was unable to take the suspense anymore.

"So, what now, Chief?"

Nathaniel sighed and turned to Jay.

"We don't have anything solid on Bo. Just a phone call. We're going to have to let him go."

Andy was about to object, and Chief Danvers held up his finger.

"You can keep him here for the full twenty-four hours if you wish, but it doesn't look like he has anything to offer. I leave it to your discretion."

Without waiting for a response, Chief Danvers returned to his office.

Andy and Jay stared at Bo in silence for quite some time. Andy turned to Jay.

"So, what are you thinking?"

Jay shook his head.

"The chief has a point. What we have is paper thin. I have no idea where to start with Bo. His story sounds believable."

Andy nodded.

"And we still have other angles to explore. I honestly think it's best to let him go. Hell, if we want to, we can always watch him from afar. I don't think he's leaving for anywhere any time soon."

Andy walked into the interrogation room and sat across from Bo.

"Thank you for your time. I just want to go over a few points in your story, and you'll be free to go."

Bo nodded.

"Alright, so you say Phil came to you to get some closure on Steve's death?"

Bo nodded.

"That's what he told me, anyway."

Andy nodded.

"And how did Phil know to come to you?"

Bo managed to keep a blank expression as he responded.

"He said Steve's uncle pointed him in my direction."

Andy's ears perked up.

"You know Doug?"

Bo slowly shook his head.

"I've only met him twice. He came looking for a job a while ago, but I didn't have anything for him. The second time was shortly after Steve died."

Bo frowned.

"He stopped by my office after what happened. He said Steve told him that if something came up, I'd be able to help. As I said, I feel partly responsible."

Andy penned down everything Bo said and nodded.

Andy asked, "What did Steve mean by that, exactly?"

"I still don't know. I'm as confused as you are with the whole thing. Two guys I never met until the past few weeks stop by asking about a kid that helped me occasionally. I don't know if I might have been the only bright spot in his life or they thought I had some of the answers to all the problems."

Andy nods, puzzled.

"Alright, I guess that's about it."

Andy rose from his seat and walked to the door. He opened it up and gestured at the exit.

"You're free to go. I'll arrange with the secretary to give you a ride back to your office."

Bo nodded and got up to leave.

"We'll let you know if we have any more questions."

Moments later, Bo took one last look at Andy before heading out of the station. Andy showed him out and then returned to his desk. With a huge sigh, he looked at Jay.

"Well, that was disappointing. I was really hoping we nabbed another man."

Jay nodded in agreement.

"The search continues, I guess."

Andy looked at his watch and frowned.

"We should get to Hillsboro Bank before it closes. We need to clear all our leads as quickly as possible."

Andy and Jay stepped into the former's vehicle and headed for Hillsboro. Jay directed Andy towards the bank, and he parked right by the entrance. The pair walked side by side, and Andy used his badge to get an audience with the bank manager.

The manager seemed to be on a call and looked up at their arrival.

"I'll have to call you back. Yeah. Keep me informed."

The bank manager looked clean-cut, with a sharp hairline and a snazzy outfit. His name plaque read 'Edward James', and he had a cheerful disposition. Mr. James smiled at his guests as he spoke.

"It's not every day that I get a visit from the police."

He extended his hands for a shake and settled into his seat.

"So, gentlemen. How can I help you?"

Andy spoke up.

"Well, Mr. James. The Steamboat Police Department is currently investigating a string of thefts that happened a few weeks ago. We recently discovered that one of the culprits had dealings with this bank."

Mr. James furrowed his eyebrows and slowly shook his head.

"That's such a shame to hear. Well, if there is any way I can aid your investigation, just let me know."

Andy nodded.

"There is. While we have apprehended two of the culprits, the money is still unaccounted for. If you could look through your bank records for any large sums deposited recently, that would be helpful."

Mr. James nodded.

"That should be easy enough to arrange. It might take some time, but I will set it as a high-priority task."

Andy and Jay rose from their seats, and the former took the bank manager's hand in a firm shake.

"Thank you for your cooperation."

Mr. James smiled and shook his head.

"Please, the honor is all mine. I'm happy to help."

The pair were escorted out of the bank, and Jay stretched once they were on the entrance sidewalk.

"That went a lot better than I anticipated."

Andy nodded in agreement.

"We're lucky the bank manager was willing to cooperate."

The two of them stepped into Andy's car and fell silent as they considered their next move.

"So, what now?" asked Jay, as he turned to Andy. Andy stroked his chin and sighed.

"Now, we head back to the station and try questioning Phil and Doug again. We should focus on finding out where the money is stashed."

Andy started his car, and the pair drove off.

☩

A few minutes later, Andy silently observed Phil from across the table. Phil didn't seem all that interested in the situation and absentmindedly cleared his ears with his pinkie. Andy spoke up.

"Were you able to get some rest?"

Phil scoffed.

"Try sleeping in that cool cell yourself. I barely closed my eyes."

Andy shook his head.

"This will be over soon enough. We just want to ask you a few more questions, and we'll schedule your arrangement hearing."

Phil waited as Andy went on.

"So, we are hell-bent on finding the missing money. If you can help us find where the cash is stashed, I am willing to help further reduce your sentence."

Phil slowly shook his head.

"Look, we've been over this already. I was the guy behind the wheel. Nothing else. How am I supposed to know where the money is?"

Andy nodded.

"I was hoping you remembered something overnight. You were in the car with them for a good amount of time. Surely, you heard something?"

Phil firmly shook his head.

"It was none of my business, so I didn't bother listening."

Andy massaged the bridge of his nose and sighed.

"Fine. I'll hear from you."

Jay escorted Phil out of the room and retrieved Doug. Andy stayed silent for a second, considering how to proceed. He leaned forward and spoke softly.

"Look, we find that money and return it to the banks, it's going to help with your sentence. You were part of the crew, so you should know where the money is stashed."

Doug slowly shook his head.

"That was Steve's job."

He leaned forward and went on.

"The agreement was that Steve would stash the majority of the cash somewhere in the Tiff mines until the heat died down."

Andy jotted that down and nodded along to the explanation.

"That's where he was on his way to when he got shot. Whether or not he managed to stash the cash, I don't know. But if you're looking for it, that's your best bet."

Andy and Jay shared a look, and the former rose from his seat.

"Give us a moment."

Andy and Jay walked out of the interrogation room and peered in through the one-way glass.

"So, do you think he's telling the truth?"

Andy shrugged.

"Honestly, I can't tell. We don't have anything else to go on. So, the Tiff mines are our best bet. The problem with that is how large the mines are. He could have hidden it anywhere. We don't have enough people to canvass the place in time."

Jay nodded.

"We can just start inch by inch and work our way through."

Andy and Jay continued to discuss their search and failed to notice Doug smiling to himself inside the interrogation room.

Days went by after that, and the first break the police force managed to make was finding Phil's cut of the stolen money. Hillsboro Bank found the money tied to an account registered under a familiar name, Steve Harris. Phil knew he was already gone, and it wouldn't get tied back to himself.

With that, they only had one-quarter of the total money stolen, but it was a start. After some more questioning, Doug and Phil were finally processed and each sentenced to seven years in prison. Neither of them made a fuss through the proceedings, and things went along rather smoothly.

The police stopped looking into Bo, and he managed to pull off his contract. It was all downhill from there for Bo. The county made good on its promise to use his land to help develop Highway 121 further south. Bo ended up with a vast expanse of cleared land and enough lot sales opportunities to keep him eyeing a near retirement.

Bo allowed the heat to die down before dipping into his share of the stolen money. With his newfound wealth, he developed a small portion of his land and built a proper office for his construction firm's new development. Months went by, and daily life in Steamboat began to settle into a sense of normalcy.

Once Bo's new office was complete, he decided it was finally time to move his old trailer. Bo stared at the trailer fondly.

"We've been through a lot together."

He pulled down some of the skirtings around the base. Backed up his truck, then hooked up the trailer and drove it away from its position. Bo glanced in his side mirror and noticed something appear from under the trailer.

"What the..."

He pulled his truck to a halt and got out of the vehicle. He walked up to the site his trailer once stood and spotted a large bag surrounded and covered with dirt.

"What is that, and how did that get there?"

Bo scanned the area as he walked up to the duffel bag. He recognized it from when Phil and Doug had come to visit him at his house. As a huge grin appeared, he knew better than to check it out in the open. Bo loaded up the bag in his truck and, after checking that he wasn't being watched, drove off with the trailer in tow.

The rest of the day was a blur to him. After relocating the trailer, he returned home and carried the duffel bag into his basement. He set it down on the coffee table and walked over to the bar to pour himself a drink.

"If that is what I think it is, I'm going to need something strong."

Bo settled in front of the coffee table and slowly opened up the duffel bag. As he unzipped the bag dust fell from the sides, staring back at him was the money neatly arranged inside. He leaned back in his chair slowly running his fingers through his hair.

"Well, shit. With this much money, it must be Doug's and Steve's cut. They already found someone's stash at another bank."

Bo stared at the money, unsure of what to do. He racked his brain for a solution and slowly nodded.

"First, to let Doug know I found his little present." After his new project was underway, Bo knew he could settle this half of these scores in his home vault without any suspicions.

⊕

Doug and Phil were both sent to Jefferson City Penitentiary. The ride there was uneventful, and the first few days were much the same. Doug already knew his way around this prison, so it wasn't hard for him to blend in. He carried Phil along for the most part, and the two prepared for what would be a long stint in jail.

A year and a half went by, and it seemed like their incarceration would last forever. On a random Tuesday, Doug sat in his jail cell, staring at the far wall, when he heard the squeals from the cart in the hall.

Doug turned and watched as one of the inmates walked up

to his cell.

"Hey, Doug. You've got mail."

Doug was surprised to hear it. He rose from his bed puzzled as if this was a mistake. The envelope was opened, as it was checked before it was to reach him. Doug retrieved the contents of the envelope, puzzled.

"A postcard?"

A custom card with Steamboat's picture on the front and the back, taped was a torn corner of a one-dollar bill. Doug smiled when he realized what he was looking at. He started to laugh, earning confused glances from the inmates around his cell. Doug whispered to himself.

"I can't wait to tell Phil. The son of a bitch found it."

ABOUT ATMOSPHERE PRESS

Atmosphere Press is an independent, full-service publisher for excellent books in all genres and for all audiences. Learn more about what we do at atmospherepress.com.

We encourage you to check out some of Atmosphere's latest releases, which are available at Amazon.com and via order from your local bookstore:

Dancing with David, a novel by Siegfried Johnson

The Friendship Quilts, a novel by June Calender

My Significant Nobody, a novel by Stevie D. Parker

Nine Days, a novel by Judy Lannon

Shadows of Robyst, a novel by K. E. Maroudas

Home Within a Landscape, a novel by Alexey L. Kovalev

Motherhood, a novel by Siamak Vakili

Death, The Pharmacist, a novel by D. Ike Horst

Mystery of the Lost Years, a novel by Bobby J. Bixler

Bone Deep Bonds, a novel by B. G. Arnold

Terriers in the Jungle, a novel by Georja Umano

Into the Emerald Dream, a novel by Autumn Allen

His Name Was Ellis, a novel by Joseph Libonati

The Cup, a novel by D. P. Hardwick

The Empathy Academy, a novel by Dustin Grinnell

Tholocco's Wake, a novel by W. W. VanOverbeke

Dying to Live, a novel by Barbara Macpherson Reyelts

Looking for Lawson, a novel by Mark Kirby

Yosef's Path: Lessons from my Father, a novel by Jane Leclere Doyle

ABOUT THE AUTHOR

Tyson was born in De Soto, Missouri a small town south of St. Louis. He began modeling at the age of 20, performing runway, fashion shows, and print ads for clients including Rawlings and Anheuser-Busch. Then he made the jump to local, regional, and national commercials. Later his antics and shenanigans led him to perform stand-up comedy in the Midwest, landing small television and independent movie roles. *Homecoming Heist* is his debut novel which matches a screenplay he wrote during the pandemic. He would like to give credit to all that have helped him along his journey.

Thank you – enjoy!